VICTIM ON TH

As the car nosed u[illegible], something moved in the National Car Park about fifty yards up, opposite Romilly Street. The car park was derelict, deserted, pot-holed, shadowy; the staff long gone home.

Across it was running a girl. Her face was bruised and dirty, her dress ripped. Her hands were tied behind her and she was gagged by a piece of sticky tape across her mouth. Desperate, bewildered, like an ill-used animal, she made a pathetic, muted sound as she stumbled and ran awkwardly, making for the car park exit and the street. Twice she tripped and fell, scraping her knees on the gravelly ground.

Miller saw her first. 'Hey, Sarge!' He nodded towards her as his foot went down hard on the pedal and he zoomed to the car park.

The Gentle Touch

Terence Feely

Based on the London Weekend Television series, THE GENTLE TOUCH, devised by Terence Feely

SPHERE BOOKS LIMITED
30-32 Gray's Inn Road, London WC1X 8JL

First published in Great Britain by Sphere Books Ltd 1981

Reprinted 1982

TRADE
MARK

Printed and bound in Great Britain by
©ollins, Glasgow

The Panda car rolled slowly through the glittering torrent of Shaftesbury Avenue, past the pleading neon blandishments of the theatre signs, the glowing shop windows full of flash suits, bizarre underwear and mind-blowing hi-fi, the paper blowing about in the gutters, the late diners on their knees for a taxi that would deign to take them home.

Constable Miller was driving. Sergeant Mick Stewart sat next to him. Both were digging into a bag of chips they had propped up on the console between them.

It had been an uneventful night. Couple of flat-out drunks, a fight in a pub at the end of Great Windmill Street; two Chinese going at each other with meat axes over in Gerrard Street.

'Not long now,' said young Miller, who was anxious to get home to a warm and willing young wife.

Stewart looked at his quartz watch, with more alarms and gadgets on it than the car itself: 'Half an hour'll see us going home to our cocoa.' He grinned: 'Oh, no, I forgot; it's not really cocoa you're interested in, is it?'

The newly married Miller sighed. He was going to have to put up with this kind of thing for a few months yet.

He swung the wheel and eased left into Dean Street, the length of it incandescent with lights spelling out invitations to every kind of entertainment known to Soho and a few that would have surprised them even in Bangkok.

As the car nosed up the street, something moved in the National Car Park about fifty yards up, opposite Romilly Street. The car park was derelict, deserted, pot-holed, shadowy; the staff long gone home.

Across it was running a girl. Her face was bruised and dirty, her dress ripped. Her hands were tied behind her and she was gagged by a piece of sticky tape across her mouth.

Desperate, bewildered, like an ill-used animal, she made a pathetic, muted sound as she stumbled and ran awkwardly, making for the car park exit and the street.

Twice she tripped and fell, scraping her knees on the gravelly ground.

Miller saw her first. 'Hey, Sarge!' He nodded towards her as his foot went down hard on the pedal and he zoomed forward to the car park.

The Panda screeched to a stop and the two policemen shot out of it as if from ejector seats.

By this time the girl had reached the car park exit and was leaning exhaustedly and hopelessly against one of the gate pillars as if expecting no succour nor solace from anyone.

As they reached her, she slumped to the ground.

The policemen bent down to her slowly. They knew that sudden movements were as sinister to a frightened human being as they were to a frightened animal.

Gently, they peeled the plaster from her mouth, quarter inch by quarter inch. Gently, they untied the stocking that fastened her wrists behind her.

And all the time they talked to her, murmured to her like fathers to a child. They were a good pair of coppers, these. They knew their jobs.

'Now then, hinny, you're all right . . .' This from the Geordie, Miller: 'You're with us, nobody can touch you now; we're going to look after you and there's nothing more to worry about.'

'Let's just get this off,' Stewart was murmuring, simultaneously. 'We'll have you right as rain in no time. You're with us now; you're safe now.'

The girl began to scream with a kind of mechanical,

regular stridency. Stewart recognised the sound. It was the body's reaction to outrage. He'd heard it from a colleague whose right arm had been blown off at the shoulder by a booby-trap car bomb. That's what he'd done after the shock had worn off and before they got the morphine into him.

'Better get her into hospital,' he said to Miller. Miller was already moving back to the car. He reached in through the window and picked up the receiver of the radio-telephone.

Detective Inspector Maggie Forbes was at home. Home was a 1930's semi-detached at Ealing with a garden at the back and a patch of lawn at the front. There was a small garage at the side, which she never used. She left her Cortina in the little drive. She usually needed to move quickly.

Maggie was in her mid-thirties. She had a mass of black curls, cornflower-blue eyes above good cheek-bones and a sensuous mouth. She had the kind of body that gave sweaters and jeans a good name and she kept it in shape in the gym.

The last thing you'd have taken her for was a Detective Inspector in the Metropolitan Police.

She was in the living room, mending her son Steve's football shirt. Steve was sixteen, with the same head of black curls as his mother. He was tall for his age, a striker in his school's football team and deadly in the air anywhere near the goalmouth. Surreptitious attempts by opponents on the blind side of the ref, to pull him down, meant that Maggie had a lot of stitching to do. He was watching TV on the other side of the room.

Maggie's father, George, was in his usual position by the fire, the inevitable newspaper in his hand. Sometimes it seemed as if newspapers grew out of

George like mushrooms. He had never been seen without one.

He read them slowly, with attention and relish, from the front page headline right through to the back, down to the tiny print at the bottom of the back page, giving the address and telephone number of the publication concerned.

He was a Cockney; a widower, retired. He'd been a porter at Covent Garden all his life and retained, in times of stress, its inventive ripeness of language. He lived around the corner in a council flat, but spent most of his time at Maggie's. He wasn't exactly in love with the police and was torn between irony and pride at his daughter's success.

And sucess it was. To make DI at just over thirty, which was when it had happened, was pretty fast moving for a man. For a woman it was phenomenal.

There were several reasons for it. She had genuine intuition. She had proved, time and time again – once to the satisfaction of the Parapsychology Unit at London University – that she consistently scored higher than chance at guessing things she could not have known rationally.

She had a good mind, quick, full of common sense. She had, when she wished to turn it on, the kind of charm that could open a Chubb safe by smiling at it. And she had a consuming detestation of crime and criminals.

This she had always had, but it had been reinforced by the brutal killing of her husband, who'd been a policeman at the same station.

He'd been blasted away by a sawn-off shotgun, trying to stop a security van being robbed and every time she looked at his picture, with its crooked smile, on the mantelpiece, she swore a silent and continuing revenge.

Her male colleagues treated her fairly. Their respect

had been hard won, but they could hardly have withheld it with a record like hers. The one exception was the man she shared an office with: Detective Inspector Bob Croft.

Normally, she'd have considered his lean, rather intense good looks highly fanciable. But he was a male chauvinist pig of Olympic calibre. He didn't believe in women in the police force. Maggie sometimes wondered where he did believe in them. In bed, probably. She had half an idea that part of his resentment against her was because she hadn't responded to the cocky expectation in his hot brown eyes when they first met.

It was George who got up from his seat by the fire and answered the telephone out in the hall. He came back immediately: 'It's for you,' he told Maggie: 'Jake Barratt.'

Jake was a Detective Sergeant on Maggie's team. She was his superior, but off-duty they were mates – he lived in the next road, was always ready to do odd jobs for her in the house if George or Steve couldn't manage; he was good with his hands.

Tonight he was on the 10 p.m. to 6 a.m. shift. He knew Maggie's mind and if he was ringing at eleven-thirty at night, she knew it was something about which she'd want to know.

'Jake?'

'It's a rape, Inspector. Nasty. Same pattern as the others. I thought you'd want to know.'

'I'll be right in.'

She put down the receiver, grabbed a coat from the peg in the hall, hurried into the living room.

She kissed both her men, briefly: 'Got to go out. Don't wait up.'

'Take care,' said Steve, casually. His father's killing

had made a mark on Steve. He concealed it well. 'Take care' was as near as he ever went to showing it and it wasn't half as casual as it sounded.

'Running around London at this time of night, it's no life for a woman,' grumbled George. 'I've said it before and – ' But the door had closed and Maggie had gone.

Maggie drove fast and confidently, no sign on her face of the delicate fluttering in the stomach that always marked the start of a case that, despite her professionalism, aroused her anger.

Rape always triggered her adrenalin; and particularly this bastard – if it was the same one. Jake had said the pattern was the same, so the odds were in its favour.

Whoever he was, he was clever, he was ruthless and he was disgusting and she was going to nail him to the wall.

She sped along half-deserted roads on the outskirts of town, the glow of Central London in the sky in front of her. It throbbed like the reflection in the clouds of some great and luminous beast, always awake, ever hungry, constantly devouring money, resources, people. Its favourite food was people. Yet she loved it. It was her city. Particularly, she loved that slice of it, its very core, which was her own; the part her station covered – from Soho, across Shaftesbury Avenue and theatreland as far as Covent Garden.

It was warm, friendly, exciting, glamorous. It was vicious, corrupt, merciless, rotten. And what gave it its special fascination was that it was all these things at once.

As Maggie sped on, in the heart of that glow in front of her, two of the city's hundreds of thousands of visitors were about to find that out. Hamish Taggart and Gordon Stewart were young, successful businessmen. They had come down from Glasgow for the international between England and Scotland. Scotland had lost.

While many of their compatriots roamed the streets in their woolly hats and interminable scarves, uttering alien oaths and looking for aggravation, Gordon and Hamish had consoled themselves with a very fine dinner at their Park Lane hotel. It had included three bottles of Chateau Rausan-Segla '69. They were now in one of the bars downstairs, looking for further diversions.

'Hey, Jimmy,' Hamish asked the barman, 'is there any action in this wee town?'

'Depends what kind you're looking for, sir,' answered the barman. 'Gambling, is it?'

'No, it is not,' answered Gordon, with a wink so powerful it nearly closed his right eye for good.

The barman, straight-faced, said nothing. He reached under the bar for something and flicked it across the counter. It was a book of matches.

Hamish picked it up. It had a picture of a girl on its glossy cover. It was expertly lit and the girl was stunning.

He opened the matchbook. Printed inside the cover were a telephone number and a name; 'Melody'.

Hamish looked at Gordon with a grin. The barman slid across the telephone and discreetly moved to the other end of the bar.

In her car Maggie was on the radio-telephone to Central Control: 'The rape: where have they taken the girl?'

'St George's Hospital, Inspector.'

'Get hold of Sergeant Fenton,' said Maggie, 'and tell him to meet me there.'

'Sergeant Fenton's off shift, Inspector,' Central Control tactfully reminded her.

'So am I,' retorted Maggie, shortly and put down the receiver.

At the hospital, young Detective Sergeant Jimmy Fenton, tousled hair the colour of a dried apricot, looking as usual as if he'd dressed from a Jumble Sale, was waiting for her in Reception. Her regular partner, he had a sleepy, slow look, which fooled everyone but Maggie. She had singled him out as a bright young jack on her first day at the station. He was unshakeably loyal to, and – although he was careful to conceal it from her – fiercely protective of Maggie.

'Hope I didn't interrupt anything important, sergeant,' she said, drily, as she strode towards him, noting his glum expression.

'Well, I was coming on nice and strong with this bird, Chief,' he said reproachfully. 'It had taken me all night to winkle her out of the disco and get her back to my pad – '

'If it's true love, there'll be other nights,' said Maggie, heartlessly. Poor Jimmy, he didn't have much luck with his love life. 'Where's the victim?' she added.

'Ward C, ma'am.'

As they hurried along the corridor, Dr Bill Ryder, the police surgeon, turned a corner in front of them and came bouncing towards them, medical bag in his hand.

He was big, solid-set, suede-shoed; a check-suited extrovert on whom you could bet to wear a blazer with a golf club badge on it at weekends. He was a florid-cheeked 38. His face lit up as he saw Maggie:

'Maggie, light of my life! How have I survived since yesterday without you?' He embraced her in a bear hug. Fenton looked on, resignedly. Maggie smiled. She knew it was all a game.

'Oh, God!' she said. 'He's been at the yeast tablets again.'

He released her with a grin.

'How is she?' she asked.

His face became serious: 'It was rape all right. A savage assault. I can guarantee you unassailable evidence if you ever catch the bastard.'

'I'll catch him,' said Maggie through closed teeth. 'What's her name?'

'Susan Ross.'

'Age?'

'Nineteen – I'll drop off all the details at the station for you.'

'Thanks, Bill. Is she seeable?'

'Well . . . remember she's just out of shock.'

'Don't worry.'

Susan Ross lay propped up on her pillows, her head and one eye covered by bandages, a purplish contusion on her left cheek, her mouth sore-looking. Her uncovered eye was closed, apparently in sleep. A uniformed policewoman was sitting beside the bed.

Maggie looked at Susan from the door, then looked sideways at Jimmy Fenton.

There were compassion and anger on his face, but she knew, in a way that she couldn't explain, that her own reaction had an added dimension that he wouldn't understand. She spoke to the WPC, snub-nosed, pale-cheeked Jenny Evans: 'Has she said anything?'

'No, ma'am.'

'All right, thank you, Evans. You can take a break.'

'Thank you, ma'am.'

She left and Maggie turned towards the bed:

'Susan?'

The closed eyes remained closed.

'Susan, my name is Detective Inspector Maggie Forbes.'

The incongruity between the title and the rather

cheeky feminine voice announcing it opened the eye. It stared at Maggie.

'I need your help,' said Maggie.

Susan kept the good eye steadily on the fine-boned face looking down at her. It was as if it were taking a long time to sink in.

She spoke finally with painful irony through bruised lips: '*You* need *my* help?'

Maggie knew all about the bitterness of rape victims. She had found that the only effective approach was flat, practical, unemotional:

'The man who attacked you,' she said; 'what happened exactly?'

Susan turned her head away: 'I don't want to think about it.'

'That's the surest way to let it mess you up,' said Maggie.

Susan turned back to her, her speech filtered through her pain: 'They've done a pretty good job of that already.'

'"They"? D'you mean there was more than one?'

Susan rolled her head away again: 'No.'

'Then what – ?'

Susan rolled her head back, looked pointedly at Jimmy Fenton, standing quietly in the corner. Maggie held Jimmy's glance: 'Wait outside, would you, sergeant?'

'Yes, guv'nor.' He'd been expecting it. He was relieved. He went quietly.

Maggie moved closer to the bed: 'Well, love?'

Susan raised herself a little: 'D'you know what they do to you when you're a rape case?' she demanded. 'D'you know what your police surgeon did to me?'

'I know the forensic procedure, yes,' said Maggie, knowing how the girl must be feeling, knowing she was hiding behind the jargon of her trade.

'"Forensic procedure",' Susan spat out through the poor, broken lips, ' – that parcels it all up nicely in a plain brown wrapper, doesn't it? The truth is it's almost as bad as the . . . the . . . thing itself. You feel like a specimen, an animal – '

Maggie allowed her face to soften: 'It must be horrible,' she admitted. 'But it's necessary. Otherwise, when we find him, we can't prove a thing in court.'

'*If* you find him.'

'The sooner you start to come through for us, the sooner we can get after him.'

Susan paused for a long time, her uncovered eye staring unblinkingly at Maggie.

Finally, she started to talk:

'My name's Susan Ross. I work in the cloakroom at the "Rendezvous" restaurant in Romilly Street; you know . . . in Soho . . .'

'What happened?'

'The last customers took a long time to go. I was late getting away . . .'

As she talked, ripples of distress started to cross her face as the reality of the scene came back to her.

She had come out of the restaurant and walked straight across to the National Car Park in Dean Street. It was just a derelict site, enclosed by wire mesh, with a small wooden cabin for the attendant. She always parked her car there. If it was after midnight they put the lights out, but left the gates open for her.

It was dark there when the lights were out, a pool of deep shadow in the heart of the shrieking neon. Especially was it dark against the back wall, where she always left her car so as not to be in anyone's way.

She had just got her keys out when she heard a kind of scrunch on the ground behind her; the sort of noise someone makes when walking on gravel. Every vestigial animal instinct told her she was in danger. She knew that, whoever it was, he was between her and her escape route through the gate. Her only chance was to turn without warning and try to dodge past him while he wasn't expecting it.

But, before she could swing round on her heel, an arm was clamped across her throat, preventing her from uttering a sound. He pointed a gun in her face with his other hand.

Then he swung her round and dragged her backwards, towards the back wall where her car was, her heels scraping uselessly on the ground.

He dragged her through a ragged, gap-toothed opening in the back wall on to another patch of waste ground behind.

It was even dimmer there than in the car park. But a sign for 'Harp' lager, flashing on and off a couple of streets away, shed a faint intermittent glow.

'Enough to see his face by?' asked Maggie, eagerly.

Susan shook her head: 'He wore a hood. And a black sweater and black trousers, that's all I can tell you. He slapped a piece of sticking plaster across my mouth – he had it all ready . . . he seemed to have everything . . . planned. I struggled like a maniac, but he was too strong and he was hitting me, hitting me . . . Then he got me down on my face and tied my hands behind me with something. Then he . . . then he . . .'

She was close to hysteria. Maggie bent over her. Christ, the kid could have been her own daughter – she was only a couple of years older than Steve!

'It's all right, love,' she murmured, 'it's all right. You're safe now.'

She stroked her face. The experienced, womanly hand lanced the hysteria and it found relief in a flood of tears:

'The worst part of it,' Susan sobbed, 'was I could . . . hear . . . people the other side . . . the other side of the wall . . . walking along the street the other side of the wall . . chattering, laughing . . . all the bright lights of Shaftesbury Avenue . . . All those people, they were only yards away . . . and I couldn't make a sound – or do a thing – to let them know what was happening to me . . . It wasn't as if it was a country lane or something . . . It was right in the middle of hundreds of people! . . .'

She started to shake uncontrollably. Maggie poured her a glass of water: 'Drink this.'

She gave Susan the glass of water then sat on the side of the bed, cradling her with an arm around her shoulders, while Susan drank it. She held the glass two-handed like a child.

Maggie waited for her to finish. She handed the glass back to Maggie, again in a curiously child-like fashion: 'Thank you,' she said, simply, calmer now.

Maggie waited for her to stop shaking completely. The hardest part was yet to come. God knows she wasn't a militant women's libber, but what *did* they do about this sort of thing before they had women police? Best to build up to it gradually . . .

'I'm sorry to do this to you, Sue, but there are a couple more things I need to know. Did he speak?'

'No, that was another awful thing,' shuddered Susan. 'He never said a word.'

'What sort of build was he?'

'Just . . . over medium height . . . very powerful.'

'And you didn't get any idea at all of the colour of his hair, eyes, nothing?'

'I told you, he had this hood on.'

It couldn't be postponed any longer. Maggie swallowed: 'And the last question – it's a dreadful question, I know that: but I've got to know. Susan . . . what, absolutely, exactly what . . . did he do to you? I mean the . . . details.'

Susan was struck silent, her mouth half open.

She made a little noise, a kind of 'Uhh – '

Maggie took both of the girl's hands gently in hers: 'It's important,' she said, softly.

Ten minutes later, Maggie was leaving the hospital with Jimmy Fenton. He queried her with his eyes:

'It's "The Frog",' she said.

'You mean he actually spoke again – and in French?' asked Jimmy.

'He didn't speak.'

She was stiff with anger, sexist anger and she knew it was wrong. The best copper was a cool copper. She concentrated on regaining that cool. Jimmy knew better than to press her until she had.

It was not until they were back in the car, on their way to the station, Jimmy driving, as usual, that he felt her vibrations slow down:

'If he didn't speak,' he asked, 'how d'you know it was "The Frog"?'

'Let's just say by his "tastes" . . . and leave it at that,' said Maggie and Jimmy sensed the vibes revving up again.

The car, blue light flashing, but no siren – Maggie would never have it used unless it was absolutely vital; she said it stopped her thinking – sped through the West End in Jimmy's skilful hands.

He had things to say and he had to say them, no matter how Maggie was feeling:

'Chief,' he resumed, 'I'm not denying it's the same man, but I mean we're so sure he's a Froggie – just because he spoke a bit of French that first time. That doesn't prove he is French. I mean I can speak a bit of the old parlez-vous myself, but that don't make me a snail-gobbler.'

Maggie clarified it in her mind as she talked: 'That's not the point,' she said. 'What I mean is this: the first time he struck, he called his victim "mon p'tit choux" – '

'"My little cabbage",' said Jimmy.

'The newspapers naturally blew it up big,' Maggie went on. 'He's raped seven times since – this will make the eighth – and never said another word. Why?'

Jimmy grinned: 'None of the other birds reminded him of cabbages.'

Maggie turned a grim face on him: 'Sergeant Fenton.'

Jimmy saw the blaze in the beautiful blue eyes: when would he learn that you didn't make jokes about rape to Maggie Forbes?

'Sorry, chief,' he said, contritely; 'I know what you're getting at. He realised that it was a dead giveaway, so he decided to keep stumm from then on.'

'Exactly,' Maggie agreed. 'Which means that he can only speak French, or English with a heavy accent.'

They had reached the station, Seven Dials. Smoke-blackened Victorian on the outside, inside it had been modernised and brought into the age of technology seven years ago.

Jimmy parked the car with his usual slide-rule precision and they went up the steps. He had not gone round and opened Maggie's door for her, nor helped her out of the car. The male–female courtesies were suspended on duty. They were strictly two coppers. It went against young Jimmy's grain, but experience had taught the Force that this was the only way it would work.

'There's a pattern we haven't seen yet,' Maggie was saying. 'I can feel it. I want the complete file on "The Frog" on my desk in ten minutes. And get me Bill Ryder if he's still here.'

'Yes, Guv'nor.'

*

Outside their hotel, Gordon and Hamish were climbing into a cab. Hamish asked for an address he had scribbled down inside the cover of the book of matches alongside the telephone number. They were chuckling and jostling each other like two schoolboys . . .

Inside Seven Dials Maggie was passing through the main CID office on her way to her own which, to her lasting dismay, she shared with Inspector Croft.

The main room was alive with noise and activity: detectives coming in from assignments, munching sandwiches from paper bags, others on their way out, typewriters clattering as reports were laboriously pecked out, telephones ringing, conversations going on.

Jake Barratt, his warm brown eyes and round face lighting up when he saw Maggie, was just putting down the telephone.

'Thanks for the call, sergeant,' she said.

'I knew it was your pond, Inspector,' said Jake. 'Good job Inspector Croft was out or he'd have moved in on it.'

'I shudder to think of Inspector Croft interrogating that poor kid,' said Maggie, grimly. She went on her way to her office.

Croft was already there. He opened up on her instantly:

'You and your team keep yourselves pretty tight,' he snapped, the lean face taut with temper.

'What's that supposed to mean?' asked Maggie.

'You're off-duty. I'm on this shift. There was no need for you to come roaring in like the Lone Ranger. I'd have been perfectly capable of handling it.'

'In the first place,' retorted Maggie, 'when was a copper ever off-duty? And in the second place, this series of rapes happens to be my case – '

'Afraid of having it solved for you, are you? – '

'And in the third place,' she interrupted, 'having you on a rape case would be like treating a burn with caustic soda.'

'Don't you mean "alleged" rape?' asked Croft.

'"Alleged"?' asked Maggie, rising, outraged to the provocation.

'Well,' said Croft, with false mildness, 'nothing's been proved yet, has it?'

'You haven't seen the state she's in!' she exclaimed, skin tightening across her cheekbones.

'Some like it rough,' said Croft and went out through the door with a malicious grin, conscious of the seething tides he would leave behind him.

As Croft left, Jimmy came in with Bill Ryder, the police surgeon.

Maggie was explosive with fury: 'That man!' she spluttered, 'that bloody man! He makes most male chauvinist pigs look like mothers' boys!'

'Maybe it would help if you looked less feminine,' suggested Ryder, straight-faced.

'And how am I supposed to do that?' she demanded.

He looked up and down her sleekly rounded body in the sweater and hip-clutching jeans: 'You could wear a dress,' he suggested, untethering his grin at last.

Maggie was not amused: 'Get wormed!' she said.

'Just a suggestion,' said Ryder urgently, nothing abashed.

Outside a luxury block of flats in Mayfair at that moment, the cab was dropping Gordon and Hamish. Hamish reached in his pocket and handed a note to the cabbie.

'Keep the – '

'Keep half the – ' interrupted Gordon.

'Change,' they said, simultaneously.

The cabbie, surly, slapped some coins into Hamish's hand and drove off, muttering. The Scotsmen went in and crossed the lobby, looking for the lifts. They had started getting exercised about the game again: 'Call it a match!' said Gordon. 'It was daylight robbery. The English should have been arrested as they came off the park!'

'They were playing thirteen men,' declared Hamish, definitively; 'I counted them!'

'And that penalty was a rip-off,' added Gordon. 'If you canna kick a man in the crutch on the football field, where can you do it?'

'The whole sport's not what it was,' said Hamish. 'It's a game now for Jessies and big girls' blouses!'

The desk in Maggie's office was covered with reports. Maggie, Jimmy and Bill Ryder were all sitting about in various stages of dishevelment:

'What we've got are eight rapes, all by the same man, yes, Bill?' said Maggie to Ryder.

Bill Ryder waved a couple of reports: 'The rapes all had the same physical . . . characteristics and . . . idiosyncrasies – yes,' he said, with a police surgeon's cautiousness.

'The same man,' said Maggie, firmly. 'And getting progressively more violent.'

She started shoving around and sorting through papers. 'The first case was a waitress, the second was a girl who worked behind the bar at a dining club. The next five . . .' She scattered the papers, trying to find the cases she wanted.

'I'm with you,' said Jimmy excitedly, 'the next five all happened near a restaurant or in restaurant areas, mainly in the suburbs.'

He found the papers Maggie had been looking for, waved them as he spoke.

Maggie snatched them from him eagerly.

Ryder spoke up: 'And this last one – the restaurant connection again.'

'If we're right about him being French,' asked Maggie, 'what does that make him?'

'Yeah – right,' said Jimmy, 'a waiter or a chef.'

Maggie thought hard: 'Up to now he's operated in the suburbs: three cases in Hendon, two in Swiss Cottage, two in Hampstead. Tonight he moved into town.'

Jimmy snapped his fingers: 'He got a job at the "Rendezvous"!'

'It's not a bad bet,' said Maggie. 'First thing tomorrow we go in there like Flint!'

'I say,' said Ryder, 'may I come? I could be of help.'

'Bill,' said Maggie kindly, 'there are no free lunches going. Anyway, as a doctor you should know – you eat too much.'

Ryder slapped his stomach indignantly: 'Not an ounce of spare flesh there!'

Hamish and Gordon had found the lifts and were now walking along the richly, cherry-red-carpeted corridor on the fifth floor, looking appreciatively at the gilded panelling that chequered the walls.

'She did say fifth floor, didn't she?' asked Gordon.

Hamish injected a growl of anticipation into his voice: 'It was the way she said it!' he answered. He reached into his pocket and took out again the match book. They both looked at the lovely, glossy face on the cover, then at each other. Their expressions were eloquent. 'Number fifty-four,' added Hamish.

A second later they were standing in front of it. They cleared their throats and straightened their ties. Gordon rang the bell. There was no reply.

'Here, let me,' said Hamish with that confidence

possessed by everyone that a bell that will not respond for anyone else on the planet will bring the desired result for them. He pressed it long and hard.

Again there was no reply.

Hamish looked at Gordon: 'She did say fifty-four, didn't she?'

'As sure as I'm standing here,' said Gordon. He tried the door. It opened. He looked again at Hamish. Hamish shrugged. They pushed the door open and walked in.

A second later they reeled out and threw up on the rich, cherry-red carpet of the corridor.

The door remained three-quarters open. Through it could be seen the backs of a pair of lovely legs and two beautifully moulded buttocks. They were streaked with blood and there was blood on the wall which one could see past them and on the carpet.

The call from the near-hysterical Scottish voice had come through to the Control Room just as Maggie was reaching her coat from the rack to go back home: the real grind would start tomorrow on the rape case. The coat went back on the peg. Murder pre-empted everything else.

Apart from other considerations, murder automatically meant a call to God; Detective Chief Inspector Russell, who had just gone to bed in his pleasant, detached house in Purley, who swore long, copiously and imaginatively and who was in Seven Dials station thirty-five minutes after climbing out of his pyjamas under the sympathetic eyes of a wife who had supported him with her common sense and loyalty throughout his career.

Bill Russell was tough, straight, with the kind of ruthlessness you need to make Detective Chief Inspector at a couple of years over forty.

It was rumoured that somewhere behind the block house jaw, the grey eyes and the skin like an old cavalry saddle there was a heart: but he had taken good care that nobody had ever glimpsed it at Seven Dials.

He brought with him into the CID room an almost tangible aura of controlled power. He spoke crisply and swiftly as usual. No one had ever heard him shout:

'Inspector Croft, get over and take charge of the team at the dead girl's flat.'

'Yes, sir' – and Croft was gone.

Russell turned and saw Maggie: 'What are you doing here, Inspector?'

'Another rape, sir. Same MO.'

'Got anything?'

'A theory.'

'Theories are for physicists. I want you on this murder with Inspector Croft.'

'But the rape – '

'There's no law that says you can't do more than one thing at a time, is there?'

Maggie allowed herself a wry smile, thinking of how many plates she was trying to keep in the air already, the piled-up case-load on her desk.

'No, sir.'

She was now in Interview Room Number One with the two Scotsmen. A detective constable was with them, taking notes. They were now very, very sober.

'What were you doing there, anyway?' asked Maggie.

'For God's sake, woman!' Hamish exploded.

Maggie's face hardened: 'Inspector,' she said, tartly.

Gordon was placatory: they were badly shaken men. 'We got her address from the barman at our hotel, Inspector.' He gestured to Hamish and Hamish produced the book of matches from his pocket, handed it to

Maggie sulkily. Maggie looked at the lovely face: she had known Melody, as she knew most of the working girls on her patch. 'We were down here on business and for the international – ' Gordon continued.

'We've told you everything we know!' Hamish exploded. 'You know everything about everything bar the boil on my backside!'

'We were the ones who reported it, remember,' said Gordon, still placatory.

'That's what you get for being a good citizen,' added Hamish. 'We could have just walked away, you know.'

Maggie decided to cool it: 'I know you could and we're grateful you didn't. She let them have her number three strength cornflower-blue smile, then put the next hard question:

'Had you ever . . . "visited" Melody before?'

Hamish started showing symptoms of imminent eruption again.

'No,' said Gordon, hurriedly.

'And you saw no one leaving as you arrived? Maybe in the lobby?'

'There wasn't a soul,' answered Gordon.

Maggie knew when the lemon had been squeezed dry; and this one had been pretty juiceless to start with. She turned decisively to the detective constable in the corner: 'Take statements from both gentlemen, check their alibis and home addresses, then give them a coffee and let them go. We got a car going anywhere near their hotel, give 'em a lift.'

'Yes, ma'am.'

She turned back to Hamish and Gordon: 'Hold yourselves free to give evidence if necessary.'

She made briskly for the door. Hamish cleared his throat, spoke mildly for the first time: 'Inspector . . .'

She could have predicted the words before they were out of his mouth.

She stopped, politely: 'Yes?'

'Is there any need for us to get in the papers?'

'Not if everything you've told us is true,' she said.

Hamish's shoulders sagged with relief: 'Thanks. Oh and . . . er . . . if it's all the same to you, we'll get a cab back to the hotel.'

Maggie smiled drily: 'Frightened of being seen in bad company?'

She left them completing their statements and went out into the CID room, plucking Jimmy Fenton after her with a flick of her head as she went through. He followed in her footsteps as she made for the door.

'Where to, chief?' he asked, as they emerged into the corridor.

'The murder flat.'

'Croft's there already.'

'So?'

Croft was coming out as they got there. He was followed by two fingerprint men and a detective constable carrying objects in plastic bags. One of them was a large, bloodstained marble ashtray.

Croft stiffened when he saw her: 'I've done everything that's necessary here,' he declared, his Scots accent stronger, as it always was when he was uptight.

'No harm in my having a look, is there?' asked Maggie, drily. 'My reports on the witnesses should be ready by the time you get back. You'll expect to have a look at those, won't you?'

Croft grunted with an ill grace and moved on.

Honest to God, thought Maggie, it was hard enough fighting villainy without having to fight your own side, too.

'That's what I like, sergeant,' she said to Jimmy, 'a nice family feeling.'

They went past the uniformed constable guarding the door and into the flat.

After a tiny vestibule, they found themselves directly in the living room. Thick, gold, curly-twist fitted carpet, little antique pieces, the waxing of centuries on them, mixed cleverly with elegant modern furniture. Two sumptuously gleaming sofas in pale lemon, a magnificent crimson begonia sitting in the middle of a glass coffee table, echoing the blood splashed on one of the walls.

Maggie was not and never would be immune to the sight of blood spilled in violence. But she forced herself to look at it and the sticky mess it had combined to make with the carpet.

She felt her anger flare again. Was it sexist anger again? she wondered. Would she have felt the same had it been a man who'd been so brutally struck down? She decided, with relief, that she would.

Jimmy Fenton had glanced at the blood as if it were so much red paint, then glanced away again, taking in the elegant room:

'Classy!'

'And houseproud,' said Maggie, running her fingers lightly over a glossily immaculate eighteenth-century escritoire.

'She wouldn't have liked all this fingerprint powder over everything,' said Jimmy. He, like Maggie, felt the lingering presence of the girl, the curious contradiction between her way of life and the ambience she had created for herself.

They went into the bedroom. The bed was huge and round with a mirrored canopy over it and a luxurious silk bedspread over it, unruffled.

It was cream, like the rest of the room, including the deep angora-soft carpet.

'Tasty!' said Jimmy.

Maggie's expressive eyes gave him one of their looks.

'Well, what I meant was,' said Jimmy, thinking fast on his feet, 'it don't look as if it was a dissatisfied customer that done her. I mean he'd hardly have made the bed up again before he left.'

But Maggie had stepped into the lavishly equipped walk-in wardrobe and was examining the expensive clothes and shoes with some curiosity. There was puzzlement on her face.

Jimmy followed her in and whistled: 'Blimey! She really was doing well!'

Maggie swung round on him, the shadow of speculation still at the back of her eyes: 'I want to have a chat with some of her colleagues,' she said. 'This is one of their favourite blocks of flats – right?'

'Yeah – must be half a dozen of them have their pads here. All class merchandise.'

'Right, so you and Tom outside round up as many as you can and get them down to the nick.'

'Gawd! All that talent, chief! I might get corrupted.'

'Sergeant,' said Maggie, sweet-and-sour, 'get cracking!'

Forty minutes later six of the choicest call girls in London were in Seven Dials police station. Three of them were with Maggie in Interview Room One, together with Jimmy and a uniformed policewoman, three were waiting for Inspector Croft in Interview Room Two, also presided over by a policewoman.

Maggie's quota consisted of Margot, Annabelle and Pauline.

Margot was classically beautiful, leggy, slinky, ginny-voiced and a smoker of gold-tipped black Russian cigarettes. She was the unofficial leader of all the girls. Annabelle was a spectacular, honey-skinned blonde with breasts of an unbelievably geometrical roundness. She affected a baby-doll innocence of voice and expression. Pauline, who was about forty-three, might have been the genteel, slightly thickening proprietress of a kiddies' dancing school.

Maggie knew them all. 'Thanks for helping to get everyone together, Margot,' said Maggie.

'Think nothing of it, darling,' drawled Margot, 'though we're all busy girls. It did take a bit of "interruptus" here and there.' She crossed her swervingly rounded legs with a swish and her black and gold silk cheong-sam fell open to the hip.

Jimmy swallowed hard.

'I've had to leave a household name tied up in a cupboard upside down,' breathed Annabelle in her best Goldilocks voice ' – and he's due to vote in the House of Commons in half an hour.'

She leaned back, the lycra of her skin-tight tiger suit taut across those perfect breasts.

Jimmy took the most intense interest in the light bulb overhead and swallowed again.

There was a general hoot of laughter, cut short by Pauline, very much the 'grande dame' in a conventional evening gown and long gloves: 'Considering what we're here to talk about,' she said, 'I think all this prep school giggling is misplaced.'

'Yes, matron,' said Margot.

Maggie took command: 'Pauline's dead right,' she said. 'I know it's mostly nerves, but let's leave it out, shall we?'

They knew Maggie. It was as if they had all sat suddenly to attention.

The girls waiting for Croft next door were getting impatient. They were Charlie, Letty and Georgia.

Charlie was the fresh-faced, tawny-haired model-girl type in a £200 iridescent green pyjama suit. Georgia was a beautiful West Indian girl with the high hips and jutting buttocks of her race, which her sprayed-on Shirley Bassey-type gown did nothing to mar. Letty looked as if she had just stepped out of a pre-war Berlin cabaret – Garboesque tails, bow tie, black tights and thigh-high boots. There was a Lesbian vibration between her and Georgia,

'I've had this,' said Georgia, making for the door at the precise moment that it opened and Croft walked in:

'Had what?' he asked.

'You name it,' said Georgia.

'I suppose you do know there's a call-out fee,' said Letty.

'Hope you've had your Vitamin E,' said Charlie.

'D'you want us all together or one at a time?' grinned Georgia.

'All right, all right!' Croft shouted, 'I've got all the comedians I can use.'

'The point is have you got all the action you can use?' queried Letty.

'I mean to say you know we'd do anything to help the police,' said Charlie.

'I once nursed the Chief Constable of you-guess-where,' said Letty.

'And he wasn't even ill,' said Georgia.

'Not until his wife found out,' said Letty.

Croft roared: 'Will you shut up!'

'Ooh, he's fierce, isn't he?' Georgia pretended to cringe.

'Will – you – shut it!' shouted Croft, red in the face.

'Better let him have his say,' said Letty. 'After all it's our necks. One of us might be next.'

'If you policemen looked after us instead of laying for

us,' said Georgia . . . 'well, no, I didn't exactly mean that as it sounded. What I meant was if you weren't on top of us all the time – '

'She didn't mean that, either,' said Letty. 'What she's trying to say – '

'In her mentally retarded way,' added Charlie.

'Charlie, for God's sake!' snapped Letty. There was needle between Charlie and Georgia, Croft noted, with his policeman's tape recorder mind. Didn't mean anything, but file it away anyway.

'All we're saying is if we got more cover from the law, this sort of thing wouldn't happen,' accused Charlie.

'Charlie, lass,' said Croft, 'you put yourself at risk the minute you go on the game. You can't blame anyone for that but yourselves. What do you want – police protection?'

'Yes!!!' they chorused. Charlie added 'Every civilisation has needed us; it's just silly to think you can win against old Mother Nature.'

'Stick it in a letter to the Home Secretary,' said Croft. 'What we're here for is to try and sort out who put Melody away.'

Georgia shivered. Letty put a hand on her shoulder.

'I agree,' said Letty, 'none of us is safe until you've found the man.'

'Or woman,' said Charlie.

'Strong woman if it was,' said Croft. 'Used a marble ashtray.'

Again Georgia shivered. All the girls looked a little sick.

'Margot, you live directly below Melody,' Maggie was asking next door. 'Did you hear anything?'

Margot shook her elegant head: 'I was over at the Hilton, making a house call.'

'There's lovely!' exclaimed Annabelle in a heavy Welsh accent.

Maggie turned to Pauline's matronly figure: 'Pauline, you're only a couple of doors away.'

'Sorry,' said Pauline, 'it's my night for my Spanish classes.'

'She's thinking of retiring to Majorca,' said Annabelle.

'Well, semi-retiring,' said Margot.

Pauline tried to bridle, but succeeded only in splitting her rosily sensible face into a broad grin.

Next door, Croft was beginning to sweat. There was something about the way these girls, professional to their beautifully groomed fingertips, projected themselves without apparently doing anything that, in the confined space of the interview room, was getting to him. He dragged his eyes away from Letty's glistening thighs, thrusting out of the top of her boots:

'Did she have any regulars?' he asked.

'Quite a few,' answered Letty, 'she was a beautiful girl.'

'You only know by seeing the same faces,' Georgia explained. 'We never talk about it. We've no idea who they were.'

'Anybody who struck you as odd?' asked Croft.

Charlie answered for them all as they pondered and shook their heads: 'No.'

In Room One, Maggie had begun to prowl, quietly, gracefully.

Jimmy read the signs. She was getting ready to pounce in some way. Suddenly, she stopped in her tracks and spoke with apparent casualness:

'Who was sharing with Melody?' she asked.

She was met by a blank wall of apparent incomprehension: 'I don't understand, darling,' Margot volunteered.

Maggie spoke with exaggerated patience, as if to children: 'Half the clothes in Melody's wardrobe were size twelve, the other half were fourteens.'

So that's what it was all about in the wardrobe, thought Jimmy.

'We all come and go, darling, you know that. We can't all be iron-willed weight-watchers,' said Margot.

'And half her shoes were sixes and the rest were eights,' Maggie came back at her.'What are you trying to tell me, our feet go in and out like the tide, too?'

Margot blew out a smoke ring, sent a smaller one spinning through it when it had expanded and watched the trick as if it were the most absorbing phenomenon she had ever seen in her life.

The others examined their jewellery, their fingernails, patted their hair.

Jimmy saw Maggie's eyes start to flash, the sensuous mouth harden, further danger signals. She started to snap out her questions:

'Where's Ruby, by the way?'

The girls sensed the change in Maggie and it disturbed them:

'Ruby . . . moved out,' offered Pauline.

'Where to?'

'We don't really go in for forwarding addresses,' said Margot. She could stand up to Maggie a little better than the rest when Maggie was turning up the heat.

'I wouldn't say you were being a great deal of help to me, would you?' asked Maggie, embracing them all in one sweeping glance, hand on her hip.

'Honestly, Maggie,' said Annabelle, sounding distressed, 'we're doing our best.'

Maggie decided she was going to get nowhere at the moment on the Ruby point and decided to change direction: 'Had Melody any enemies that you know of?'

'Only, you might say, the common enemy,' said Margot.

Agreement dawned on Annabelle's face: 'That's right! They were always pitching into each other.'

'Who was that?'

'Come on, Maggie dear,' drawled Margot, 'it's not like you to be slow over the jumps.'

'Jeremy Miller?' said Maggie.

Next door, Croft, using his own style and a different approach, had just reached the same point:

'Jeremy Miller putting on the pressure for more money in return for seeing you're not bothered by his fellow-scum, is that what you're saying?'

'That's exactly what we're saying,' said Letty, 'and Melody howled louder than any of us. And if ever any of this came up in court, I'd suffer from total amnesia.'

'No, it's not the pimp's style,' said Croft. 'Might ruin his white gloves.'

'We're not saying he did it personally,' said Georgia. She shifted her shapely rump on to the edge of the table and he found his concentration wandering again.

Letty rescued him: 'Why don't you roast him anyway?' she suggested. 'He deserves it.'

'Letty, I'll do my job,' said Croft, 'and you do yours. Okay?'

'Sounds a sensible arrangement,' retorted Letty. 'Frankly, I don't think you'd stand much chance the other way around.'

'Funny lady,' said Croft. 'Thanks for the cabaret.'

'Any time you want a private audition . . .' said Letty, in her smokiest Marlene Dietrich voice.

'I'll send an officer in to take your statements,' said Croft, biting down on the words as if he were chopping them off a length of metal, 'then you can go.'

He made a quick exit, jerking his head at the policewoman, who followed him.

The girls took out their hand mirrors:

'Odd, isn't it,' said Charlie, carefully renovating her shapely mouth.

'What?' asked Georgia, looking up from her mirror, knowing something was coming.

'How nobody mentioned how you and Melody got up each other's noses.'

Georgia laid down her mirror with great deliberation: 'Look, we may not have got on, but if you think I could kill anyone, you're more bent than I thought.'

'*I'm* bent!' said Charlie, with a laugh.

'Just shut it!' shouted Georgia. She brought her fist down with great force on to the table, knocking off the metal ashtray.

Letty moved to her and touched her soothingly on the arm.

The door opened and a detective constable entered.

The girls became beautiful waxworks.

In Room One, Maggie was winding up, too: 'Anyone know what Melody was really called?'

Margot shrugged: 'Like the man said, all the customers want is girls with nice teeth and no last names.'

'If you think of anything that *might* help,' said Maggie, with a glitteringly sarcastic smile which she privately thought was a little unfair, 'you know where to find me.' She turned to Jimmy: 'Right, sergeant. Take down their – '. Before she could articulate 'statements', she was drowned in a politely orchestrated, but nevertheless raucous cheer. She left.

Jimmy wiped his forehead with his handkerchief and sat down with pad and pen: 'Right then,' he said, in a tone of counterfeit command he was far from feeling, 'let's be having you.' Even as the words were leaving his mouth he could have bitten off his tongue . . .

Half an hour later he joined Maggie in her office. It was two in the morning, but their adrenalin was high: 'I've compared notes with Inspector Croft,' said Maggie. 'We both agree. Possible pointer to Jeremy Miller.'

'Mr Suave himself,' said Jimmy. 'If he got any smoother he'd slide right out of his Jermyn Street shirt. And what about Ruby? They knew more about her than they were saying – '

'I'd swear she was sharing with Melody,' said Maggie. 'We've got her on file, I want her picture buzzed around. She shouldn't be hard to find. I seem to remember she was rather spectacular.'

Jimmy sat there going through his notes: 'The rundown on the flat and the body. No credit cards, no cheque books, no passport, driving licence, nothing that might give us a clue to Melody's real identity.'

Maggie agreed: 'Apart from her fingerprints, it's almost as if whoever killed her wanted her wiped off the face of the city.'

'That's what I thought,' said Jimmy, 'but I asked Tommy Evans – you know those X-ray eyes of his – well, I asked him to do one last search of the flat and he came up with this.'

He pulled a crumpled envelope out of his jeans pocket, tried to smooth it out, gave it to Maggie.

It was addressed to 'Miss Julia Portman'. The address

was indecipherable.

'Julia Portman . . . Could be her real name, d'you think?'

'Well, nobody's really called Melody, chief – know what I mean? It was stuffed down the side of the sofa, like maybe she was choked about it.'

'No sign of the letter in it, I suppose?' asked Maggie.

'I couldn't get that lucky, Inspector. I mean, it wasn't in me stars.'

'Then you're going to have to do a bit of plodding, then aren't you?' said Maggie.

'I was afraid, you was going to say that,' said Jimmy.

'D'you know, sergeant,' responded Maggie, 'sometimes your intuition frightens me.'

Her lips twitched at the mask of resignation that settled over Jimmy's straight, English-Cockney features, topped by the weird apricot hair: 'Just for now,' she said, 'let's go and have a talk with Mr Jeremy Miller.'

'How d'you know Croft hasn't already done it?'

'Because I know Miller's latest address and I happen to know that Inspector Croft doesn't.'

Forty minutes later, Maggie was knocking on Detective Chief Inspector Russell's door.

'Come!' shouted Russell.

As she went in, she heard Croft who was standing in front of the seated Russell's desk: 'Miller is favourite to have done it according to the girls. Could be.'

'You talked to him?' asked Russell.

'We're just tracing him,' answered Croft.

'He hasn't been home all night,' said Maggie, impulsively. As she saw Croft's face tighten, she realised that she had inflicted a totally unintended humiliation on him. She was briefly sorry, but then she remembered that there was a bastard to catch and small considerations of personal pride couldn't matter less.

Russell felt the same. Unless they disrupted the efficiency of his operation he didn't give a damn about internecine rivalries.

'Sit down,' he commanded both of them.

They sat.

'Know who the girl really was?' Russell asked.

'No, sir, there's something odd there,' said Maggie. 'Someone had scrubbed her.'

'Didn't the other tarts know?' asked Russell. No euphemisms about call-girls for Russell, thought Maggie; a tart was a tart was a tart.

'You know the girls, sir,' said Croft. '"Anonymous is beautiful".'

'Sergeant Fenton may have a lead. He's following it up,' said Maggie.

'And we'll stay on Miller,' said Croft. 'He does lean on the girls.'

'Then there's a girl who's gone missing,' added Maggie. 'I've got a feeling she's tied into this somewhere.'

'Feminine intuition,' said Croft, trying to enlist Russell in an all-guys-together joke.

Russell put him down, his face as impassive as an Easter Island statue: 'How's the Hatton Garden job?' he asked him.

Croft's face straightened: 'It's coming slowly, sir.'

'Mortimer Street?' asked Russell of Maggie.

'We've got some information coming,' she told him.

'Keep me in touch,' said Russell.

'Yes, sir,' they promised.

'And if you need any more manpower on the rapist, let me know,' he said to Maggie.

'I will, sir.'

'All right.' He dismissed them with the tiniest inflection of his features.

Maggie and Croft made to go, then Maggie stopped

and riffled in her pocket: 'Oh . . .' she said '. . . I tore this out of a magazine in the hairdressers. It's about a new therapy for . . . you know . . . spastics.' Russells's elder son was a cadet in the Navy: his younger one was a spastic in a special hospital. 'They've had good results in – '

He cut her story short by putting out his hand for it: 'I'll read it,' he said and put it in a drawer.

Maggie and Croft went, Maggie a little awkwardly.

Out in the corridor Croft turned to Maggie, a sneer in the hot brown eyes: 'That's what I like about women,' he said, '– their winning little ways.'

'Inspector Croft,' said Maggie wearily, 'why don't you stick it in your ear?'

She went to get her topcoat from the office, left and climbed into her car. This time of night it shouldn't take her more than twenty minutes to Ealing.

In his office, Russell was putting on his topcoat, too. He made for the door, stopped halfway, then went back to his desk.

He took out the article Maggie had given him and slipped it in his pocket.

Maggie parked the Cortina in the little drive and let herself in. She was puzzled to see light coming from the living room.

Cautiously, she pushed open the door. All the lights were on, but there was no one to be seen.

There was a rustle and her father's head popped up on the other side of the table. He looked dishevelled and exasperated.

'Dad!' she exclaimed. 'What are you doing here? Have you any idea what time it is?'

'Of course I have!' he said, in a shouted whisper, 'it's three o'clock in the bloody morning, that's what bloody time it is!'

'Then why aren't you at home in bed?'

'I'm trying to make our Steve's bloody costume,' George replied. 'They're doing a story about "Everard and Heloise" in the school play, remember? – '

'"Abelard and Heloise"!' Maggie corrected him.

'I don't care if it's bacon lard and Heloise, you were supposed to be making his monk's habit and you haven't done a thing about it. I could tell tonight he was getting a bit worried, so I got stuck in – '

'God! It completely slipped my mind!' said Maggie, her hand to a brow that was pounding with headache.

'Too busy ridding the country of villainy,' said George.

'Dad, leave it out, will you, just for once. I'm stuck with a murder now as well as a rape *and* I'm sharing the murder with Croft, which doesn't make things any easier. Anyway, let's see how far you've got.'

George slowly and shamefacedly rose from the floor, hauling up with him a confusion of paper patterns, trailing cotton and brown cloth.

The habit looked like a grotesque joke by Salvador Dali. One sleeve was about four feet long, the other about one foot. The hem was like a Big Dipper and the whole thing was about the size of a tent.

Maggie battled to keep a straight face, but the combination of George's acutely embarrassed face and the bizarre garment itself was too much for her and her weariness was washed away in a flood of laughter, in which George eventually joined.

She crossed and threw her arms about him, still laughing: 'Oh, Dad, you're a caution!'

'Well . . .' said George, ruefully.

'Leave it to me,' she said, 'I'll finish it tomorrow night. And it's too late for you to go tramping home, you'd better sleep in the spare room.'

She kissed him and made for the door.

'Maggie,' he said, 'you won't have time tomorrow night – you'll get caught up again, you know you will.'

'Dad,' she said, suddenly dog-tired again, 'I'm on early turn tomorrow – I just want to sack out; right? 'Night, love.'

She went out into the hall. Her father shook his head at her shapely, retreating back.

Upstairs, she peeped in at Steve, who was out to the world, that familiar, surprised expression on his face, as if he was astonished to find himself asleep at all. Then she went to her own room, took two aspirins, scrubbed her teeth, wiped off her sparse make-up and passed out almost before she'd climbed into her nightgown.

She slept as if anaesthetised for four and a half hours. At seven-thirty a.m. she was in the kitchen, a piece of toast in one hand, a duster in the other, occasionally sipping from a mug of tea standing on the breakfast bar. She dusted without pattern, or design, her mind preoccupied with the problems of the day ahead.

Her father was perched on a high stool, newspaper in one hand, mug of tea in the other:

'Your case is in here,' he said. '"Girl about twenty-three, so far unidentified . . ." Makes it difficult, dunnit?'

'Yes, it does,' admitted Maggie. 'Still, it's early yet – we might get her identified today.' She crossed to look over his shoulder.

Steve came loping into the room, the lunatic monk's habit draped all around him and swamping him, trailing on the floor like a wet sail.

'Mum,' he said, reaching for the cereal box, 'I'm supposed to be Abelard, not Quasimodo.'

Maggie glanced sideways at George: 'I know, love. It's only a mock-up.'

'Looks more like a cock-up,' said Steve, slashing milk on to his heaped bowl of cereal.

'Less of that,' said Maggie. 'And sit down to eat your breakfast. I don't want bits all over the floor.'

Steve took off the habit and sat at the breakfast bar. While the garment was over his head she took the sneaky opportunity to wipe up some crumbs she herself had shed on the floor from her toast.

'You are coming to see the play, Mum, aren't you?' asked Steve, mouth stuffed with processed wheat.

'Of course I am, love. Friday, isn't it?'

Steve groaned: 'Thursday! I knew you'd forget.'

'I won't forget, honest! And don't gobble! I've told you before.'

'I'm late, Mum. Nobody called me,' Steve complained.

George took it up on Maggie's behalf: 'Your mother didn't get in till just about dawn this morning. Anyway, when I was your age I was getting myself up, summer or winter, hail or shine. You're all too soft, that's what's wrong with you kids today.'

As George made his speech Steve, who knew it by heart, silently mouthed each well-worn word a fraction of a second before his granddad said it.

He thought George, behind him, hadn't noticed until George expertly skeeted a drinks mat at him, catching him neatly behind the ear.

'Thanks, granddad,' said Steve sourly. 'You should take up the discus, only when you throw it, don't let go.'

'Steve, don't be rude to your grandfather,' said Maggie. 'And Dad, you're as bad as he is.' She poured herself another half cup of tea. Steve emptied some more cereal into his bowl.

'Anyway, Mum,' he said, 'you've got to be there to give me moral support. This play, it's been written by the English master. You should hear some of the stuff he's given me to rabbit: "Whenas the stars that punctuate the night their glitter lend our souls – "'

'Prob'ly sounds a lot better without your mouth full,' said Maggie, shaking her duster out of the window.

'Don't count on it,' Steve replied. He shook his head in wonderment: 'That's the sort of stuff they teach us, then they wonder why we grow up to be weirdos.'

Maggie folded her duster and put it away in a drawer: 'You were a weirdo in your pram,' she said.

'There's more of the muck,' said Steve, 'listen: "And then in that dark vale where no man treads – "'. Maggie suddenly swooped on him and started plucking at him, at his shirt collar and his cuffs:

'Did you *have* to put this on?' she demanded. 'You've got other shirts that aren't frayed.'

'No, Mum,' said Steve, 'they're all dirty.'

'Well *tell* me when they're dirty – you're not dumb, are you?'

'I'll bung them in the machine today,' George offered.

'Would you, Dad?' said Maggie. 'You're a treasure. Oh, and could you get some eggs? Number Threes. Got to go. I'll hear the rest tonight, Steve.'

'You're pretty safe there,' said Steve, 'you're never home in time.'

'I will be, I promise,' said Maggie.

'And you definitely will be there for the play?'

'Cross my heart. Now I really must beat it, loves. Be good.' She gave them both a quick kiss. ''Bye, Steve! 'Bye, Dad!'

''Bye, Mum.'

''Bye, love. Keep the streets safe for an old soldier.'

And Maggie was gone.

As she turned on to the old A40, in the hulking shadow

of the M4 motorway, she pondered the question that never let a day go by without plaguing her. Was she being fair to Steve? He no longer had a father – the villains had seen to that. Now he was in danger of not having a mother, either; the villains were seeing to that, too. Police hours were ferocious and the three-shift system a joke. Crime recognised no frontiers, no armistices, least of all a copper's knocking-off time. You simply couldn't walk off a case at six o'clock at night because it happened to be going-home time. If there was a lead to be followed, you had to follow it. If there was a grass who couldn't meet you until ten o'clock at night, you met him. And if what he told you took you to a raunchy Soho club at two in the morning, among the poached eyes of the men and the desperate mouths of the women, you'd be there.

And even when you'd finally managed to cut loose and get home, there was no guarantee you were going to be able to stay there. A break or a new development on a case could happen at any time and once you'd made inspector and it was your case, the buck stopped with you. You had to get off your backside and dive back in even if what you really wanted to do was to drop unconscious.

Perhaps her father was right; that it was no job for a woman. But, then, was it a job for anyone? You weren't really appreciated; you were always looked at a bit sideways. She'd once seen one of her women colleagues in the uniformed branch being beaten up by two drunks. A crowd was standing by, watching, but not one of them lifted a finger to help the girl. It was Maggie, rocketing out of the car in which she was passing, like an avenging angel – a trained and fit avenging angel with no noble sentiments about fighting fair against scum – who had rescued her colleague.

Afterwards, she had given the crowd a highly

flavoured opinion of them that would have scorched the ears off an elephant. One of or two of them had the good grace to look ashamed. But only one or two.

Then there were the lawyers, the operators among them who specialised in defending their clients by defaming and smearing the police, branding them as liars, venal and corrupt, doing their best to destroy their credibility in the eyes of the jury.

They were just doing their job, of course. But what kind of a job *was* that? And how could they take the money for doing it – a hell of a lot of money, too – knowing where it had come from?

She went round Hogarth Roundabout, just avoiding getting crushed by a 40-ton juggernaut. The driver winked at her. She'd give him a bloody wink if she had the time!

Even her neighbours had an ambivalent attitude towards her. They were always a bit wary when she was around, a bit sarky. 'Once a policeman always a policeman' was a favourite saying in her district, with its implication that you couldn't ever really make friends with a copper; he'd pull you in as soon as look at you if you ever gave him the chance.

It was only her stunning good looks, which were the kind that seemed to appeal to women as much as to men, that redressed the balance in some measure and brought her a level of acceptance. That and the quick tongue she inherited from her Cockney father. Nobody ever outquipped Maggie and most people had by now learned not to try.

Did people really want the law? Did they really want the police? Did they want to be protected against the arrogant thugs to whom the rest of the population were 'mugs', human cattle put on earth for the sole purpose of providing them with a fat and easy living?

At demos and trades union disputes the police caught

it from both sides. Sworn at, kicked and beaten with impartiality by opposing factions, they were the only ones who couldn't win.

Trying to prevent people from maiming each other, they usually ended the day with the highest percentage of walking wounded and some of them flat on stretchers, being accused of 'brutality' by everyone, especially by those who weren't there.

Once, in her uniformed days, Maggie remembered being on demo duty. She had seen a bearded youth felled by a stick wielded by the opposition. She had plunged in and dragged him to safety at the side of the road. He spat in her face: 'Keep out of it, pig!' he said. Then, as his dazed senses returned, he corrected himself: 'Sorry!' he said, 'I meant sow!'

Most of these irritations and wounds she shared, of course, with her male colleagues. But there was one thing they couldn't share. She was a copper, yes. But she was also a widow with a home to run and an adolescent son to bring up.

The Force recognised the problem, but could do nothing about it except in the negative sense that, had she had two children instead of one, she would have to resign, the judgement being that another child would be the critical overload.

She worried it, chewed it, ground it in the gears of her sharpened mind as she did at some time each day, or sometimes late at night when she'd have preferred to sleep.

Was Steve suffering? Why did she stay with the job? Was it really to avenge her dead husband? A sense of mission? A hatred of criminals? Or was it simply that she loved it; the constant challenge to her wits, her will, her courage?

She drew in to the kerb outside Seven Dials almost as neatly as Jimmy, the ace, might have done and as always the problem was instantly buried in the immediate preoccupations of the day.

In the CID room, Jimmy Fenton was already there. For some reason it always irritated her when he beat her to it, even though he did only live in Earl's Court and cheated by using a bicycle; perhaps it was because she was damned sure he took a secret delight in it. He put his hand over the mouthpiece of his telephone as she came in.

'What we got?' she fired at him. He looked tired, she thought. But then he always did, until he got into a violent situation, when he was like an exploding power station.

'Jeremy Miller's back home,' he said. 'Got him on the line.'

'Let him sweat,' Maggie told him. 'Tell him we'll be round to see him later and he's not to set foot outside the door until we get there.'

Jimmy passed on the message and put down the telephone. He got up from his chair, dried-apricot hair a mess, clothes looking as if they needed burning – even though she knew he was fanatically clean. If Steve looked like that, she reflected, she'd throw a fit. But this, among other things, was what made Jimmy a good detective: he simply didn't look like one.

'Where – ' he started.

'Did the good word come on the Mortimer Street furs job?' she interrupted.

'There's a report from Sergeant Barratt on your desk, chief. His snout came up trumps. I should think we'll be feeling a few collars before the week's out.'

'Terrific!' said Maggie. Already the adrenalin was beginning to flow. This was what she was in it for. The sheer, bloody . . . what? Oh, sod it! She jerked her head at Jimmy and he followed her through to her office.

'Where's Inspector Croft?' she asked.

'He was just going off shift when he got a lead on the Hatton Garden job and he went after it.'

Maggie breathed a silent sigh of relief. At least she wasn't going to have to cope with Croft this morning.

'By the way,' she grinned, 'how'd it go with your bird when you went back last night – if you went back?'

'I did,' he said, 'and . . . well . . . that time of the morning . . . she elbowed me, didn't she.'

'Oh, dear, nowhere painful, I hope.' Swiftly, as they talked, she was reading through the most vital of the heap of reports piled up on her blotter.

'Listen, chief,' said Jimmy, 'it's not funny. I've got a fragile ego. A woman palmist told me that.'

'She must have been drunk,' said Maggie, cheerfully.

'Thanks,' said Jimmy. 'Like some coffee?'

'No, thank you, sergeant,' she said decisively, pushing the pile of reports from one side of her desk to the other. 'There's nothing there that can't wait. Let's get on with it.'

'Jeremy Miller?' he asked, expectantly.

He was right, of course, she thought. Murder had to take precedence over rape. But the hell with precedence. She was going to follow her feelings: 'No,' she said. 'I told you, Miller can sweat for a bit. I want to hit that restaurant where Susan worked – "The Rendezvous".'

She started out of the door and stopped: 'Oh, and remind me to get some shirts for Steve.'

'Will do.'

'The Rendezvous' was one of those excellent, small, discreet Soho restaurants, which make no fuss, never advertise, never lose their rating in the guide books and provide a soothing of the spirit and the stomach for actors, businessmen, lawyers, MPs and agents trying to damp down their clients' paranoia.

The ambience was cool, the eye caught traces of fresh greenery wherever one looked and there were always pretty girls.

It was at its best at lunchtime on a hot day when patrons walked off a pavement baking like a Provençal oven into an embrace of hushed coolness that seemed to rest on the marble tiles like the water in a swimming pool.

It was hot today. June had suddenly decided to happen. Maggie and Fenton scrambled gratefully out of the car, dodged the swatches of water with which a waiter, already at this early hour, was laving and freshening the immediate environs of the premises and went in, into the coolness and the chaos.

The staff were starting to lay the covers for lunch. There was an air of purposeful frenzy. Why so early? wondered Maggie. Then she remembered, wistfully, the few occasions when she had been able to squeeze in a dinner party when her husband was alive and how the time seemed to fly. She found herself thinking of that kind of thing at the most inconvenient times.

Eventually, they isolated Franco, the proprietor, by the simple process of picking on the one who was shouting the loudest.

Maggie showed him her warrant card. He bowed, his Italian accent heavy; his black hair shimmering: 'Si, Signora Inspettore, Franco Angelo at your service. Whatta can I do for you?'

'You can drop the plastic Italiano for a start,' said Maggie, her eyes flashing with amusement, 'you're no more Franco Angelo than I'm Maggie Forbesiano. East Ham?'

Brown-eyed, olive-skinned Franco, every inch a Neapolitan, instantly reverted to his native Cockney, grinning wildly:

'Double top!' he shouted. 'Frank Angel's the name. How d'you rumble me?'

'I was most likely born in the next street,' said Maggie. 'Can't you tell?'

'Well, yeah, but – '

'It's about your cashier, Susan Ross,' said Jimmy. He and Maggie had this technique: they kept people off balance by alternating their questions, taking different directions. Innocent or guilty, it was amazing how much more information it produced from people.

Frank's face dropped: 'Terrible! Bloody terrible!' he said. 'That poor kid. I tell you, this town's becoming a battlefield. How can you expect people to come for a nice, quiet night out – '

'Have you taken on any new waiters lately?' Maggie interrupted abruptly.

Frank Angel looked from Maggie to Jimmy, then back again, realisation dawning on his face: 'Here . . . you don't think? – '

He broke off to shout at a waiter: 'You can get another cover on there – close up the settings. Space is money!'

He turned back to Maggie and Jimmy: 'No, no . . . I haven't. But you don't really think – '

'Any new staff at all?' asked Jimmy.

'One, in the kitchens,' said Frank, continuing to look puzzled; 'a commis chef. I hired him last week.'

'Is he French?' asked Jimmy.

Frank Angel looked in bewilderment from one to the other: 'Yes, he is,' he said. 'Look, what is all this? – '

'Name?'

'Jacques Lapra.'

'Is he in now?' asked Maggie.

'Yeah,' said Frank.

'Lead the way.'

Forgetting, for once, to do his Italian maitre d' walk, he led them through into his spotless kitchens with their scrubbed pine tables and huge, gleaming utensils.

Here there was a kind of disciplined chaos with sous-chefs and commis-chefs chopping, slicing, boning, sawing and gutting, a pastry-chef rolling dough, a sauces-chef proceeding as delicately as an alchemist.

As Maggie came into shot there was a blizzard of wolf whistles, howls and comments in a variety of accents:

'Bellissima! . . .'

'I'd like to get that on my pastry board! . . .'

'I wouldn't stuff that with chestnuts! . . .'

'You don't get many of those to a portion! . . .'

Normally, Maggie would have been amused. Today, perhaps because of the nature of her mission, she was not.

Her eyes darkened to the colour of a thunderhead and she held up her warrant card:

'Shut it!' she said, unceremoniously.

There was an instant and uneasy silence. Jimmy came to stand beside her. Frank Angel stood behind.

'Which of you is Jacques Lapra?' she demanded.

He stepped forward in his apron, a cleaver still in his hand. There was blood on his apron: 'I am Jacques Lapra. What do you want with me?'

He was big, hulking. His facial appearance and long, black sideboards would not make him a reassuring companion in a dark alley.

'I'm Detective Inspector Forbes. You've heard about Susan Ross being attacked.'

'The girl in the garde-robe? Certainly. But . . .'

He shrugged and looked helplessly at Frank Angel.

Frank shrugged back.

'Please understand,' Maggie reassured Lapra, 'nobody suspects you of anything. But it's possible a Frenchman was involved in the attack, so we're checking any Frenchmen at Susan's place of work. That seems sensible, don't you think?'

'That is logical, yes,' said Lapra, 'but it could not have been me last night.'

'Why not?' asked Jimmy.

'I was here all night from five o'clock. I was still clearing up until after one o'clock in the morning.'

Frank chipped in: 'That's right, he was. This business is like an iceberg – seven eighths of it the public never sees.'

Without warning, another French voice opened up like an artillery barrage behind them: a voice full of amazement and fury:

'*Merde et merde et merde et merde!*' it roared.

Maggie, Jimmy and Frank Angel turned round. Standing there like a rotund, medium-sized, apoplectic bull, which had somehow contrived to go bright red in the face, was a man in a suit with unmistakably Continental shoulders and the kind of Homburg-style hat favoured by small-town French Rotarians.

'What is this,' continued the apparition, 'an 'oliday camp or a kitchen? I go to 'ave a tooth filled and when I come back, what do I find? – '

'This is Monsieur Turot,' Frank interrupted hastily; 'he's our Head Chef.' He lifted his eyes to heaven: 'A genius!' he added, with shameless sycophancy. Angel knew a treasure when he had one. He wasn't going to lose Turot for want of a little crawling.

But Turot was not to be appeased. He simply carried on as if Frank hadn't uttered: 'My kitchen overflowing with strangers, my staff sitting on their behind parts – '

Maggie ignored him for the moment and turned to Frank Angel:

'I thought you said you had only one French employee.'

Turot pushed himself forward so that she was forced to confront his empurpled face. He spoke with pained restraint and dignity: 'I am not French, madame, I am Belgian. And who "le diable", might I ask , are you?'

Maggie showed him her warrant card. It had a

marvellously sedative effect on the Belgian: 'What time did you leave last night?' she asked.

'Ah! The unfortunate affair of the little cloakroom girl,' said the Belgian.

'He sounds like Hercules Poirot,' Jimmy said to Maggie, sotto voce, out of the corner of his mouth.

'What time did you leave?' Maggie repeated.

'Early,' said Turot, 'about a quarter to eleven. Last orders had been taken.'

'Did you go straight home?' queried Jimmy.

The carmine in Turot's face, which had been ebbing away, rose again in tandem with his indignation: 'May I ask what business that is of yours?' he demanded.

'It's nothing personal, Pierre,' Frank Angel assured him anxiously.

Turot, as usual, ignored him, rounding instead on Jimmy: 'Do I look like the type,' he demanded, 'who goes round fornicating the little cloakroom girls?'

'It's not that, it's not that,' said Frank, the peace-maker, hastily. 'It's got something to do with accents. You see, the man who done it had a French accent.'

'So we're checking everyone with a French accent. Got it?' added Jimmy.

'To the British,' responded Turot, crushingly, 'all accents are French – and niggers begin now at Bayswater.' He shrugged, somehow dismissing both the British and the French to some rubbish tip of the mind: '*Néanmoins*,' he added, 'what was the question?'

'You heard,' said Jimmy. Continental creep.

'No,' said Turot, with a hint of defiance, 'I did not go straight home.'

'Oh?' said Maggie, the monosyllable carrying a world of interest.

'There is nothing for me at home just now' said Turot. Was there a hint of sadness there? 'I went first to a little club. I stayed until two o'clock.'

'Name of the club?' asked Jimmy.

'The Green Man.'

'Did anyone see you there?' asked Maggie.

Turot made a little bow. His words seemed to hold some hidden significance: 'Madam, I think you will have no difficulty in establishing my presence there.'

'I hope not, Hercules,' said Jimmy. 'Otherwise we might have to come round and blow down your ear again. Know what I mean?'

'Thank you for your co-operation,' said Maggie,'and thank you, Mr Angel. I hope we won't have to bother you again.' All the same, she had that funny feeling and it was telling her that, somehow, they would. She turned on her heel and went, followed by Jimmy and Frank Angel.

Turot rounded on his staff, who had been watching, fascinated spectators, the interrogation of their tyrant:

'So what are you staring at? Get on with your pitiful version of lunch. It may not be fit for human consumption, but maybe you will get lucky and the customers will bring their dogs!'

Frank Angel was out in Romilly Street, closing Maggie's car door:

'If you ever feel like a bite, there'll always be a table for you here, Inspector. And,' with an ingratiating wink, this, 'I don't think you'll find the bill too crippling.'

'Thanks,' said Maggie with a brief smile, 'but I've got to watch my figure.' She wished she had a quid for every meal ticket she'd been offered in Soho. But start taking favours and you felt obliged to repay them. Maggie didn't believe in feeling obliged to anyone.

Jimmy piloted them up Romilly Street: 'How d'you reckon Turot?' she asked him.

'I wouldn't rule the fat berk out,' replied Jimmy. 'And I'll bet he makes a lousy omelette.'

Maggie grinned: 'That's just because he had a go at you.'

'Prob'ly,' said Jimmy, cheerfully, winning a battle of wills with a brewery truck coming the other way. 'Where now? "The Green Man"?'

'No, let's give them an hour to get their eyes ungummed. I think we'll go and shake down Master Jeremy Miller.'

Jimmy swung round into Old Compton Street, suddenly jinked half right, spun the wheel and screeched to a stop on the corner of Berwick Street where the market was already in full cry, the road crammed with stalls, a miniature Petticoat Lane in the middle of London's West End, selling everything from fruit to Chinese incense.

'What? – ' asked Maggie, momentarily at a loss.

'Shirts,' said Jimmy. 'Steve for the use of.'

'Thanks, sergeant,' she smiled. She got out and plunged into the frothing mass of people.

Jimmy stayed with the car. He wouldn't put it past some joker to half-inch it if he left it unguarded around here.

Maggie made her way through the crush to a clothes stall halfway down the street.

'Hello, Ron!' she said to the dark, wiry little man who ran it.

'Maggie, love! What's new?'

Ron Howell had a double value to Maggie. Not only did he sell good quality clothes at fair prices, he also had a talent for intelligence. He was one of her sharpest-eyed, keenest-eared informants:

'Murder,' said Maggie. 'Rape. Nothing much new about either of them.' She turned over the merchandise like any other housewife as they talked.

'I heard,' said Ron.

'Know anything?'

''Fraid not. Early days. Now if it was about that jewellers in Jermyn Street . . .'

'I'm interested,' said Maggie.

'Could have something on it for you tomorrow.'

'Ta. Oh! Haven't seen "Red" Ruby around, have you?'

'Bought her a drink in the "Fenwick" last night. Seemed a bit shook up. Said she was heading south.'

'Did she say where, exactly?'

'Sorry.'

'Never mind – thanks, Ron. That's one I owe you.'

'Forget it,' said Ron. 'Anything else I can do for you?'

'God!' said Maggie, 'I almost forgot! Shirts for Steve. You know his size. Whatever your own lads would fancy.'

'Got just the thing,' said Ron, the serious salesman now. 'Marvellous quality, ridiculous price!'

'I know,' grinned Maggie, '– they fell off the back of Shaw Taylor's Range Rover.'

She paid for the shirts, took them back to the car: 'All right, sergeant,' she said, 'let's have Mr Miller.'

While Jimmy started to punch his way through the knotted mid-morning traffic to Hill Street, Mayfair, where Miller had his flat, Maggie was busy on the radio to Central Control.

She asked for Ruby's description to be circulated and a particular watch kept on southern ports and airports. Ruby's sudden take-off had made her more convinced than ever that she'd been sharing with Melody and was somehow connected with her murder.

'Did you get anywhere with that envelope,' she asked, as they settled for the one-way system round Piccadilly and the Haymarket, 'the one with Julia Portman on it?'

'I thought you'd never ask, Chief,' grinned Jimmy. 'I got to thinking why should she have it? Must be her real name – right?' He swerved to avoid hitting an obvious pot-head, who leaped over the railings around Eros in front of him. 'Postmark "Sidcup". Flash! Was it from a friend? Could she have lived there at one time – Melody, I mean. So I put one of the night lads on to looking up old electoral registers for Sidcup – '

'Give me the bottom line, sergeant,' said Maggie.

'Mr Gerald and Mrs Agatha Portman, Gledhill Road, Sidcup,' he said, triumphantly.

'Her parents?'

'Got to be,' said Jimmy, 'we couldn't be that unlucky.'

'Right,' said Maggie, 'so it's Miller first, then "The Green Man" to check Turot's alibi, then the Portmans.'

Jimmy cleared his throat: 'I didn't . . . like . . . hear anything about lunch in that schedule, chief.'

'Stop off and buy yourself a Mars bar,' grinned Maggie, heartlessly.

Jimmy sighed. Once Maggie really started to motor on a case, she stopped for nothing. A rapist on the loose would have been bad enough – but a rapist and a murder! Well, Croft was on the murder, too, so maybe he'd take some of the strain, but Maggie wouldn't rely on that. Still, there wasn't another Guv'nor on the Force he'd rather work for.

They rang the bell by the side of the solid mahogany door of Miller's flat. It was opened by a tall, languorous blonde of a stunning patrician elegance. She was wearing a yellow track suit with a little Hermes apron over it. In her left hand, she dangled a fresh fish by its tail.

She ushered them straight in, knowing instantly who they were, although they had never met each other before.

The living room was a monument to undeclared income and good taste. There was a rosy Aubusson carpet on the gleaming parquet floor, a nicely judged conversation piece of two gold velvet armchairs and a sofa, modern but classic in style, facing the Empire fireplace. The walls were covered by a neutral-shaded serge cloth against which gilt-framed pictures, including at least two exquisite Bonnard nudes, glowed with colour. A wall sized plate-glass window overlooked an exotic indoor garden and in front of it stood a table littered casually with lacquered and enamelled snuff-boxes and Fabergé trinkets.

'I've just come back from the market with this,' announced the blonde, without preamble, holding up the fish. 'I'm giving him my speciality for luncheon – "Sole Bonne Femme".'

'You're his new live-in Bonne Femme, are you?' asked Jimmy.

'I'm his status symbol,' she said. 'They made his life hell at Eton so he gets his revenge by keeping a Peer's daughter.'

'What's your excuse?' asked Maggie.

'I love the slimy slug,' she said. '"Nostalgie de la boue".'

'Where is he?' asked Maggie. 'He was told to be here.'

'He's in his study,' said the blonde. 'I'll get him.'

'Study!' snorted Jimmy. 'What's he writing, "Crime For Beginners"?'

Two minutes later, Miller came in alone. He was African, about thirty, with a pale coffee skin and a civilised cruel face.

He was wearing a white silk shirt and white trousers, a heavy gold medallion hanging from a chain around his neck:

'Maggie, my dear girl,' he declared, 'I swear you get younger by the hour.'

'Take no notice,' said Maggie to Jimmy, 'he records all the old Cary Grant movies off telelvision and plays them back to himself like Linguaphone lessons.'

She turned to Miller: 'I'm glad you stayed in,' she said, a hint of aggression in her tone.

'Anything to oblige a lady,' answered Miller. 'I presume you're asking for my help on the killing of that unfortunate girl. Terrible . . .'

'Where were you last night?' asked Maggie.

He lit a long brown cigarette with elaborate casualness: 'Always straight to the point. Direct. I like that in a woman,' he said.

'Why don't you try it yourself?' asked Maggie. 'And do switch off the charm. It has about the same effect on me as a cold Chinese dinner.'

They were old adversaries, these two. Maggie knew that Miller was one of the biggest, unconvicted thugs in London and he knew that she was one of the best detectives on the Force.

Sometimes it happened, in a situation of this kind, that a sort of mutual respect grew up between the two antagonists. Not with these two. Beneath the banter there was real dislike. And Miller had a fear amounting almost to superstition that, if ever he fell, it would be Maggie who brought him down.

Nevertheless, he continued to smile: 'Sharp as ever! I was at a little club I own in Greek Street. Trouble with the accounts.' He wiggled his elegant fingers: 'Little hands in the till.'

'Cut 'em off, did you?' asked Jimmy, drily. Miller affected him like sewer gas. He'd also found he could get under the silky coffee skin.

Miller ignored him and went on addressing Maggie:

'Everybody saw me there. Why? Where would you like me to have been?'

'The girl who was murdered last night was one of

yours,' said Maggie. 'You're everyone's favourite suspect.'

Miller raised his hands in the air in a gesture of bewilderment: 'One of *my* girls? What am I, a schoolteacher?'

'I dare say you do have to do a little of that, too,' said Maggie, her eyes sparking. 'I'd say your curriculum must be rather bizarre, mind you.'

Miller coughed out a short, dry laugh: 'Entertaining lady. If ever you leave the Force – '

'We'll send you an exploding telegram,' Jimmy interrupted.

Miller's voice was patient and reasonable: 'I protect working girls against exploitation and violence – help them to get on with their jobs.'

'I bet you help old women across the street, too,' said Maggie.

'Only if they don't want to go,' added Jimmy.

Maggie changed tack suddenly: 'What did you and Melody fight about?'

'We didn't fight,' said Miller, as if astonished, 'I was very fond of the girl!'

'We've got witnesses who'll say otherwise.'

'What witnesses would they be?'

'None of your business – yet. How much was she paying you for protection against others of your kind?'

'I don't think I remember mentioning that she paid me anything,' said Miller, stretching luxuriously on the long, gold sofa like a cat. 'We social workers don't look for payment, we see it as part of our duty to our fellow man. Of course, the girls are very grateful and very generous and if they sometimes give me a little present, it would be churlish to refuse it – don't you think?'

Maggie's voice took on a cutting edge: 'Tell me, Miller, when did the Fire Department last give your clubs and other little rat-runs a really good going over?'

Miller uncurled himself from the sofa with a quick movement which he managed not to make look hasty. He had abandoned the bantering tone. Now he was debating: 'Look,' he said, spreading his hands, 'if I'm really what you say I am and if this girl was paying me a fortune for protection, why should I kill the golden goose?'

'Any number of reasons,' said Maggie. 'A quarrel over raising the level of her "gifts" to you. Maybe she knew something about you, something about your other activities. Maybe she was going to shop you. What did you say the name of that club was?'

'I didn't,' said Miller.

'No, you didn't,' said Jimmy, ostentatiously getting out his notebook.

'That's right,' said Miller.

'But you will,' said Maggie, 'otherwise we'll have to continue this little chat down the station.'

Miller choked back his rising temper: 'It's called "The Trap Door".'

'Why don't you try falling through it?' suggested Jimmy.

'Look here,' said Miller, losing his cool at last and swinging up from the sofa, 'I don't have to take this from your monkey!'

He turned to Jimmy: 'If only you were better educated, I could insult you,' he said.

'Give it a go,' said Jimmy.

'It's no good,' said Miller. 'It would be like fighting a duel with a blind man.'

'You'd end up with a white stick right up your nostril,' said Jimmy.

Miller opened his mouth to reply, but Maggie shut him up· 'Don't go on any holidays just now,' she said.

Then she and Jimmy were gone.

Miller picked up the telephone, dialled a number viciously, as if he could hurt the receiver: 'Tommy?' he said. 'Get your arse round here. We've got some calls to make.'

As they drove away from the flats, Maggie was on the radio to Central Control at Seven Dials: 'I want every member of the staff of "The Trap Door" questioned. I want to know if Miller was there all night. I want to know if he left at any time and came back later and I want to know what those times were. Over and out.'

'The Green Man' turned out to be a small, chic club in Frith Street, very well turned out and obviously gay. A representative assortment of its clientele was already at the bar. They ranged from the full macho leather-with-one-earring, through the sparrow-like effeminate, to the full-moustached tweedy. The barman was totally bald with Dr Spock eyebrows. To Maggie's suppressed but intense amusement, it was Jimmy, with his extraordinary hair, who attracted all the attention as he and Maggie went in.

They made pigeon-like 'Nnn' and 'Ooh' cooing, about him:

'Nnn . . . anyone order apricot flan?' asked Sparrow.

'She brought her sister with her,' said Leather.

'That's not her sister,' boomed Tweedy; 'it's a friend who's had the operation.'

'No,' said Sparrow, observantly, 'there's no silicone there. It all moves about.'

Maggie and Jimmy waited patiently and with good humour, noting the discreetly private dining cubicles and the Leonardo prints of sketches of the male body around the walls.

'Floor show finished, is it?' asked Maggie, finally. She

flashed her warrant card. 'Then perhaps we can get down to business.'

Instantly, the camp was largely discarded and they became serious:

'Sorry, Inspector,' said Sparrow, 'it's just that it's been a dull morning.' He tossed his head at the barman: 'And her Bloody Mary's have been vicious! How can we help?'

'Geezer by the name of Turot,' said Jimmy. 'Belgian. Claims he was here between ten thirty and two last night. Anyone see him?'

'I did,' said Tweedy. 'Always comes in after work. Doesn't like to go home.'

'It's since his friend died,' said Leather. 'Poor bastard. They'd been together twenty years.' He said it as if it were a kind of record.

'It's called Fidelity,' Sparrow told him, with hidden needle there somewhere. 'You can't even spell it.'

'Some people can spell everything and do sod-all about anything,' Leather came back at him.

'Anyone else see him?' asked Maggie.

'Yes, I did,' said Leather.

'And me,' said Sparrow.

'And he was here all the time, didn't leave until two?' asked Maggie. She looked at the barman. He nodded with great authority.

'Yeah . . . well, thanks, fellers,' said Jimmy.

Sparrow laughed appreciatively: 'Fellers! I haven't been called that in a long time.'

'Don't be greedy,' said Leather, 'you've been called practically everything else.'

He looked for applause to Maggie and Jimmy, but they had gone.

'Well, guv,' said Jimmy as they walked slowly back to the car, the sun now hot on their backs, 'I'd say we didn't even hit the crossbar with Hercules Poirot.'

'I'd say we weren't even in the right park,' agreed Maggie.

'What now?' asked Jimmy.

'There's French in the case,' said Maggie. We do what the French do – go back to Psychology.'

'Hey?' said Jimmy.

'Back to the station,' said Maggie.

'I thought we were going to Sidcup.'

'I want some guidance from Bill Ryder. I know he had to be in court this morning, so he'll probably be at Seven Dials before he goes back to his practice.'

There was silence for a moment. Jimmy was thoughtful as he drove. Then he said 'We'll probably find Bill Ryder in "The Tank".'

'The Tank' was the station's local pub, all brass, glowing plush and polished woodwork. They went there to relax after a hard day. A lot of them preferred its food, too, to that of the station's canteen; maybe it was just the atmosphere they preferred.

'Yes, I should think he'll be in "The Tank",' agreed Maggie.

'Having his lunch,' said Jimmy.

'Most likely,' she said, her mouth beginning to twitch, although she continued to look straight ahead, as he did.

'Well, then,' said Jimmy, developing his thesis as carefully as if he were shooting for a degree, 'seeing as we're pushed for time we wouldn't be wasting any if we had a bite to eat with him while we talked.'

Maggie, whose feminine instincts would never have allowed young Jimmy to go without his lunch anyway, whatever she might say, pretended to have been won over by his logic:

'All right, sergeant,' she smiled, 'you've convinced me. You get lunch.'

Jimmy, whose usual breakfast consisted of brushing

his teeth with a cornflake, sent up a prayer of thanks to the patron saint of detective sergeants and sent down a message of hope to his stomach, which was beginning to growl like a hungry tiger.

At the same time as 'Tommy', who'd had to get in from East Ham, was joining Jeremy Miller in his flat, Georgia, Letty, Charlie, Pauline and Annabelle were joining Margot in hers.

Like her, the flat was elegant and different. The ceramic tiled entrance hall was ablaze with flowers and a balcony opposite the front door overlooked the living room one floor down, which one reached by way of a delicate, airy, practically invisibly-flown staircase. It was down these stairs that the girls were now clattering, all in jeans, shepherded by Margot.

Margot was in a slim, long, soft wool morning gown, slit at the front to a strategic point just above the knee and with a cowl that fell back over her slender, shapely shoulders. It was an elusive peach colour, which looked sensational against her Thirties-style furniture – huge, blocky armchairs and sofas in whitey-cream wool with just one huge, purple bean bag.

There were masses of flowers down here, too, filling the room with their scent and triggering, momentarily, in some of the girls, echoes of and regrets for an innocence that seemed to belong to another life.

'You know where the drinks are,' said Margot, 'help yourselves.'

'I need one,' said Letty. 'There's still a policeman on Melody's door. Uniforms give me the creeps.'

'I thought they were one of your specialities, Letty,' said Pauline, ironically.

'Only when she's wearing them,' added Annabelle. 'Where's the tonic?'

'Where it always is,' said Margot, 'on the shelf.'

'You should know, darling,' said Letty to Annabelle, scratching back, 'that's where you were all last week.'

'My clientele was out of town,' retorted Annabelle, blandly.

'So I hear,' Letty came back, 'all in the same geriatric clinic in Zurich.'

'Oh, dear!' said Annabelle, grimly. She abandoned making her drink and started towards Letty.

Pauline casually interposed her substantial figure between them: 'I do think it's so unproductive to quarrel among ourselves when we've all got a common cause, don't you?' she asked, with her sweetly insincere, headmistress's smile. 'Who's got the brandy?'

Georgia handed her a shot, adding ginger ale for her, too: 'I'm psychic,' she said.

'Georgia, you're a doll,' said Pauline, gratefully.

'Press her tummy and she'll say "Papa",' said Charlie.

'Just so long as it isn't "Mama",' answered Georgia.

They had now all got their drinks and Margot took charge with her customary cool authority: 'Now that we've all finished taking out our nerves on each other, shall we sit down?'

The girls arranged themselves around the room, Letty and Georgia brushing against each other as usual.

'Now then,' Margot continued, ' – and I don't want any bullshit – I take it we can all accept that none of us killed Melody.'

'No, of course we didn't!' Letty exploded, horrified.

'She was a lovely kid,' commented Pauline.

'If that's what the police think, they're sick – '

'I don't think they do,' said Margot, damping down the outcry.

She paused and looked around at them one by one: 'Okay. Now what about Ruby?'

There was a silence.

'Well?' asked Margot.

'What about Ruby?' asked Letty. 'That can mean a lot of things.'

'Margot – ' Charlie began.

'I'm not asking anyone what they know,' Margot explained, carefully.

'Melody and Ruby were like sisters,' said Charlie, 'we all know that . . . she wouldn't – '

Margot intervened: 'I've said, darling. I don't want to know. If anyone has anything to say, just don't. Not to me. Not to each other.' She paused. 'Not to the police.'

'We wouldn't, anyway,' said Georgia.

'It's not Ruby we have to keep quiet about,' said Charlie, with a half-glance at Georgia.

'I've told you – shut it!' said Georgia.

'I don't see why I should,' said Charlie. 'You beat her up and we all know it.'

'Bloody rubbish!' shouted Georgia. 'I slapped her face for calling me a golliwog. That's as far as it went. And you've been stirring it ever since, you poisonous – '

'I hate to sound callous about it,' Pauline interrupted, graciously, 'but surely we're wasting a great opportunity here, aren't we? Instead of rowing among ourselves, shouldn't we really be talking about the chance that's now been presented to us to get rid of J. Miller, Esq., Eton, Magdalen and Wormwood Scrubs?'

The front door bell rang. The girls looked at each other like the Macbeths listening to the knocking on the castle door.

Margot went over to her door telephone: 'Who is it?'

They all heard the reply: 'It's Jeremy Miller. Open the door.'

'It's . . . it's inconvenient at the moment,' said Margot.

'Oh, stop pissing about,' came the reply. 'I've brought my little friend Tommy with me and he's beginning to lean on the door. I hate to think what will happen if he leans any harder.'

Margot looked at the other girls, shrugged and pressed the button that opened the door.

They all looked up as Miller and Tommy, his 'minder', came down the stairs.

Tommy exuded physical intimidation. He was built like a concrete gun emplacement, his neck was as wide as his head and his face had the ugliness of the simpleton sadist.

'Tread lightly, would you, Tommy dear,' said Margot. 'I'd hate you to come through the stairs and break my floor.'

Tommy came on down the stairs and walked at her with the impartiality of a car-crusher about to crumple a saloon.

'Tommy,' said Miller, quietly and the walking disaster area stopped and stayed where he was.

Miller had added a white jacket to the white shirt and trousers he was wearing earlier.

'I wonder why your sort wears such a lot of white?' asked Margot. 'Is it a compensation for what you're like inside?'

'My sort?' asked Miller, ominously, thinking it was a racial put-down.

'Pimps, procurers, thugs, that sort of person,' she explained, easily.

'It reflects our purity of heart,' answered Miller, relaxing. 'Tell me, which one of you suggested I had Melody killed?'

'All of us,' said Charlie.

'That's right,' said Letty. 'It was an idea that occurred to us all simultaneously. Funny, isn't it? I wonder why that was?'

'You dreary trollops,' he said. 'What have I ever done to you?'

'Just bled us white, black Dracula, sweetheart,' replied Georgia.

Miller nodded to Tommy, who moved towards Georgia menacingly: 'But don't damage the goods,' said Miller, as the hulk raised a great paw.

Instead of hitting her, he gripped a pressure point between her neck and shoulder, making her scream with pain.

'Ingratitude,' said Miller. 'If there's one thing that hurts me it's that. I keep all those ill-bred thugs away from you for the tiniest of considerations. I don't force you to work – '

'Don't be a bloody hypocrite!' said Annabelle. 'It's when we try to stop that we're in trouble!'

They all shouted their agreement. 'That's right . . . absolutely right . . . just try getting out!' they yelled.

'Do keep it down, would you,' asked Miller, gently ironic. 'Think of the neighbours.'

'Is that why Melody died?' demanded Letty – 'because she told you she was giving up?'

Miller nodded at Tommy again and this time he gave Letty the neck-press treatment.

Letty groaned with pain.

'You cowardly pig!' shouted Charlie. 'You can't even do your own hurting – even when it's girls, can you?'

Miller secretly marvelled at the courage of these girls. With an animal like Tommy standing over them, knowing what he could do to them, how much he could hurt – and even damage if Miller gave the word – they still sauced him, they still fought back. They refused to become the broken-spirited automata he would so much have liked them to be, for a quiet life.

Perhaps it was time to teach them a lesson: give them a real fright.

He considered for a moment, then looked around unhurriedly at face after face, including Letty and Georgia, who were obviously still in distress from Tommy's ministrations and who were comforting each other.

He allowed a pause to develop.

The girls watched him. Miller had great presence, when he chose; great sinister presence, which was heightened by his elegant appearance and exquisite voice and the effect was chilling.

He spoke now, theatrically, his voice silky with menace:

'It would be amusing . . . It would be amusing, would it not, if you'd got it right? It would be amusing if it were I who . . . dispensed . . . with Melody. Because she was beginning to be a bore: because she was more trouble than she was worth. Because a barking bitch is best put down!' The last sentence was delivered with the hiss and crack of a whip.

Then he looked around at the faces again, letting the words sink in.

He was pleased to see the shaken expressions on their faces.

Then, without warning, he was suddenly shocked out of his shoes himself.

From somewhere behind him, a Scottish voice said: 'I'll buy that!'

Miller spun around as if he'd taken an arrow in the back.

There, coming blandly down the stairs, unhurried and enjoying himself was Inspector Bob Croft, his detective sergeant remaining on the balcony above, looking down. Croft was still talking as he came down the stairs:

'I find that very plausible,' he said. 'I'd like to chat with you about that down the station.'

He came steadily on into the room, froze the uncertainly advancing Tommy with a hard brown eye: 'Don't do it, laddie,' he said, 'or I'll personally throw the key in the river that locks you away for good.'

Tommy stopped moving.

'What the hell are you doing here?' hissed Miller. He hated being surprised. He hated even more being physically shocked. It affected his stomach.

'If you don't mind me saying so,' Croft replied amicably, 'that's not the question you should be asking. You should be asking can you ring your lawyer.'

Miller looked about him as if he would find the answer somewhere in the atmosphere:

'Don't be absurd!' he said. 'I was just joking!'

'Oh?' said Croft. He turned to Georgia. She was still rubbing the sore point on her shoulder:

'Did you think he was joking?'

'No,' she said with a kind of bitter enthusiasm.

Croft next turned to Letty, also massaging the painful place where Tommy had hurt her:

'Did you?'

'No,' said Letty, triumphantly staring at Miller.

Croft faced Miller, a grim smile on his face:

'Nobody seems to think you were joking, chummy. I think we'd better continue this conversation down the nick.'

It was the humiliation of it all, in front of the girls, that scoured Miller's ego worst of all. They were watching a demonstration of the fact that he was not all-powerful, not the elegant, untouchable son of Satan he liked to be thought, but a common crook, who could he hauled off to the nick just like any of them.

'You charge me with mur . . . with anything,' he snarled, 'and I'll have your pension.'

'Good thinking,' said Croft. He pointed to Letty and then to Georgia. 'Assault will do for now, I think.'

'You've slipped a gear,' said Miller. 'You can't be serious.'

'Solemn,' said Croft.

Maggie and Jimmy had been stuck in one of those traffic jams that, conceived by a computer somewhere at Traffic Division, New Scotland Yard, are totally impossible for the wit of man to unravel. Jimmy, with all his knowledge of the back-doubles, an esoteric piece of learning in which he could compete with any cab-driver, even he couldn't beat it.

He tried going behind it, side-tracking it, making a wide semi-circle around it, but each time, at the end of the street by which they thought they had made their escape, there was the immovable knot of metal and the tumult of drivers, their blood boiling as well as their radiators, going quietly rabid in their motorised cells. And over everything, the sun beat mercilessly down in one of those London days when it can suddenly turn into Europe's hottest capital and typists rush to plunge their bare bottoms into the Serpentine at lunchtime.

All Maggie and Jimmy wanted when they got back to Seven Dials was to lave their throats with a cold lager, then grab Bill Ryder.

What they got as they went up the steps was Jeremy Miller, vicious and triumphant, coming down them:

'What have you been doing here?' asked Maggie, shortly.

Miller was at his most mocking: 'Your esteemed colleague Inspector Croft pulled me in for questioning on the Melody murder. Meanwhile, your team had come up with the All Clear on my alibi, so he had to let me go. You know, you geniuses ought to get your skulls sorted out. Otherwise, the taxpayers are going to be asking for their money back. In fact, I'd be first in the queue.' He grinned whitely and strode cockily off down the street.

What made it worse was that there was not a sparkle of sweat on his matt brown skin.

Maggie and Jimmy mopped their brows and looked at each other. They didn't have to say anything. They both knew that Maggie was for it. And Croft.

They went through to the CID room. There was a scent of expectancy in the air. A sergeant came to Maggie: 'Ma'am, Chief Inspector Russell – '

'Wants to see me,' she interrupted. 'Now there's a surprise!'

She cut a swathe through the room on her way to Russell's office. Jimmy sat down at his desk. A dozen pairs of inquisitive eyes swivelled towards him. He shrugged his shoulder, fed up.

In his functional, Adam-green office along the corridor, Russell was being withering in his disgust:

'It's made the whole station look like bloody fools! The prime rule: when you're on a case double-handed, keep in touch!'

'It's not easy, sir,' said Maggie. 'We're both working on other cases besides this one. I've got the tape – '

Russell rode over her: 'Mrs Forbes, I don't need to be told by you the case-load this station carries. I still expect elementary procedures to be carried out. I've a bloody good mind to send you both back to college for a refresher course!'

'If Inspector Forbes had told me Miller was claiming an alibi I'd never have pulled him in,' claimed Croft.

'Sergeant Fenton and I tried to raise you four times on the RT,' Maggie accused Forbes. 'Yours was never manned.'

'I've got better things to do than to wait for the radio to squawk –and so has my servant.'

All the time, Russell was watching with the wise and

merciless grey eyes, almost as if he were in cover and they couldn't see him. He had this capacity for stillness, so that you forgot him. Many a villain had found to his cost that Russell could kid you he wasn't really there.

'You didn't even *try* to contact me,' Maggie accused Croft.

'There was no point, for God's sake!' He ran his hand through his hair in indignation which he considered to be righteous: 'I wasn't after Miller. I wanted to talk to Margot – '

'I'd already told you what she had to say; *all* she had to say – '

'I thought it was just possible,' answered Croft, sarcastically, 'that there was something Wonder Woman Forbes had forgotten to ask.'

Russell had seen and heard enough. He came out of the undergrowth:

'Let's leave out the comedy, shall we?' he said to Croft. 'What's your explanation?'

Croft explained, under strain, as everyone was when they'd boobed and had to face the unyielding Russell countenance: 'As I said, sir, I wanted to see the woman, Margot. As I got to her flat I saw Miller and his heavy going in. I had the porter let me in quietly. It was all off the cuff, the whole thing.'

He turned to Maggie, a sceptical register creeping into his voice: 'Anyway, how good is Miller's alibi?' he asked.

Maggie stiffened: 'I think you can take it I know how to check an alibi,' she said. God help me, she thought, if we weren't standing in front of Russell, I'd let this sod have one straight across the Adam's Apple.

'Just trying to keep in touch,' said Croft, with a smirk.

'Don't be infantile!' she told him.

Russell somehow fixed their attention on him without saying a word and without even rising from his seat. His voice was not harsh or ranting, just firm and quiet. But somehow it gave you gooseflesh right down the back of your arms.

'I want to tell you two something,' he said, 'and I want you to listen, because I shan't be saying it again. I don't care what kind of kindergarten sex-war you carry on off-duty, but if I get so much as a sniff of an idea that it's affecting your work, you'll find yourselves back in uniform so fast you won't know what time it is. You're both good coppers and I don't want to lose you, but if I have to, I will. Got it?'

'Yes, sir,' they said, simultaneously.

Russell transferred his attention to Croft: 'How's Hatton Garden coming?'

'One last push and I think I can crack it, sir.'

'And the container truck hi-jackings?'

'We've got a lead. We think we know where the goods are transferred. It should be just a question of timing now.'

'Good. I want those two. Drop everything else and stay with them.'

'*Everything* else, sir?'

'Yes,' answered Russell, equably and it would have taken an extremely imprudent man to take the matter further.

Russell now transferred his attention to Maggie: 'Forbes, I want you to stay with the murder and the rape. I want those two badly as well.'

'Yes, sir,' said Maggie.

'But – ' started Croft.

'That's all,' said Russell. And when Russell said that was all, it was.

They hesitated, almost imperceptibly, then went.

They walked along the corridor in stiff silence until they reached their office, then Croft unleashed his dammed-up frustration:

'Satisfied?' he exploded. 'Got the murder all to yourself now?'

'Don't be thick!' she said. 'Maybe you don't realise it, but we've just been tactfully "segregated" like a couple of squabbling schoolkids who can't be trusted not to sit next to each other in class. Perhaps you don't feel humiliated by that – well, I do!'

'I'll bet!' said Croft. He picked up some files and slammed out of the office.

Maggie sat down wearily. To tell the truth, she'd have been perfectly happy to let Croft have the murder so that she would be free – well, comparatively free; she riffled through the files on her desk – to concentrate on the rapist.

All right, Melody was dead and had been killed savagely, which was terrible. But she *was* dead. These other girls, the victims of the rapist, were alive, but things had been done to them which would stay with them every living moment, which could perhaps ruin the lives they had to live; which could poison their relationships with men for ever.

And this bastard, whoever he was, was still around. He'd already ravaged eight victims . . . nine? How many more?

She picked up the telephone: 'Inspector Forbes here. Can you find out for me, please, if Dr Ryder is still in the building?'

Ten minutes later, she and Jimmy were sitting in 'The Tank'. Jimmy had a look of muted ecstasy on his face. In front of him were two enormous ham-and-salad rolls, French-style. Maggie had a couple of egg sandwiches. Dr Ryder was pushing his way towards them through the crowd with three pints.

Ryder had already been in there for some time and was feeling no pain: 'Maggie,' he declaimed, as he put the drinks down on the table, 'why don't you let me take you away from all this? You should be at the Colombe d'Or in perpetual sunshine, sipping a mimosa, waiting for caviar followed by a steak au poivre, not sinking dirty great pints in this place!'

'Well, who's buying me the dirty great pints?' asked Maggie. 'I'll have a mimosa. Go on – go and ask Jack to make me a mimosa.'

Bill Ryder laughed, his bluff called: 'Ah, well, you have to have the touch, you know.'

Maggie took a reflective sip of her pint: 'You know it's funny how we keep talking about restaurants. They've run right through this case. Don't you find that odd, Jimmy?' In here all bets were off, rank was dropped and first names only were used. It was astonishing how therapeutic it could be – and creative. There was a school of thought that claimed more crimes were solved in 'The Tank' than in the station itself.

Jimmy was lost in the rapture of climbing outside his gargantuan French sandwiches.

'I said don't you find that odd?' she repeated.

'Erry Ogg,' he said, his mouth stuffed with bread, ham, lettuce, tomato and cucumber in one glorious palate-thrilling, stomach-caressing bundle.

'What I mean is,' said Maggie, taking a small bite out of her sandwich, 'that restaurants have played some part or other in every incident. What if our rapist were a restaurant freak?'

Jimmy swallowed monumentally, clearing the passages and organs for speech:

'You mean he doesn't necessarily work in one, he just goes to them a lot?'

'It would fit the picture just as well,' said Maggie. 'What do you think, Bill?'

Jimmy took the opportunity to reload his facial cavity.

'It could make sense,' said Bill. 'Food and drink are

the oldest aphrodisiacs in the world. Some men get very horny after a good meal.'

Jimmy spoke, muffled, through his latest mouthful: 'Better take that sandwich away from him, Maggie,' he warned.

'Jimmy, shut up,' said Maggie. She turned to Ryder again. 'Go on, Bill,' she asked. 'Suppose our man is like that. Why does it have to be rape?'

Bill took a considered swig of his beer. Slightly high he might have been, but it was amazing how an appeal to his professional opinion could concentrate his mind: 'Lots of reasons,' he said. 'He may be the kind of man who can only relate to women superficially . . . what I mean really is primitively . . . Well, what I really mean is that there are certain men who literally don't see anything else in a woman but one specific thing. Well, our man could be one of those.'

'Yes, I see,' said Maggie. Bill took a swig of his beer. Jimmy had finished off his first sandwich, was taking a deeply satisfied breath before starting on his second.

'On the other hand,' Bill went on. Oh God, thought Maggie, here come the qualifications, the ifs and buts: doctors, lawyers, accountants, they were all the same; none of them was capable of giving a straight answer to a straight question.

'On the other hand, what, Bill?' she asked, with a barely repressed sigh.

'Well, I'm sorry,' he said, sensing her mood, 'but it is a very complex subject and I'm not a psychiatrist, just a simple, run-of-the-mill physician.'

'Cut the modesty trip and let's have it,' said Maggie.

'Well, it could be that he feels guilty about sex, unsure of himself, or that it's dirty, that kind of thing. That would mean that he could only make it anonymously, as it were.'

‘Does he have a type?’ asked Maggie.

‘Not necessarily,’ Bill replied. ‘He’s driven by need; or fantasy. Or he might suddenly see something he fancies; or it might simply be availability, whatever’s there.’ He sipped his beer again, then went on: ‘Sometimes, yes, they may have a type that tends to recur – maybe they have an ideal that’s unattainable, so they take anyone who looks a bit like her. Or maybe they’re just hooked on a particular kind of look.’

During all this Jimmy had stopped chewing. Yet he remained very silent.

‘Yes, all right, I see. Well thanks, Bill,’ said Maggie, finally.

‘For you, Maggie. Any time. How’s the murder going? D’you know who the girl is yet?’

‘Keeping our fingers crossed,’ said Maggie. ‘We hope we’ve located her parents, but we won’t know until the Slowest Eater in the West here has finished his disgustingly over-sized lunch.’

‘I enjoy my food!’ mumbled Jimmy, through a tightly packed mouth.’

‘Yeah, well enjoy the rest of that in the car,’ said Maggie, ‘we’re on our way.’

Jimmy grabbed the uneaten half of his second sandwich and hurried after her through the door:

‘Nice to talk to you, Doc,’ he said. Bill carefully brushed off the blizzard of crumbs with which he’d been bombarded as Jimmy’s back disappeared.

Jimmy drove skilfully, one-handed, while he continued steadily to demolish the remainder of his jumbo-sized sandwich, which he held in the other. Maggie studied him, her head on one side:

‘Traffic would have you if they caught you driving like that,’ she said, contemplatively.

‘Traffic make dead sure they get their proper time off for refreshments,’ said Jimmy. ‘What do we see if ever we manage to get up to the canteen? It's stuffed to the walls with Bimboes in baggy pants and goggles, putting the nosh away like they've heard there's going to be a famine. I'll tell you something, guv'nor; if there is, they're the ones who are going to cause it!'

Maggie smiled, but her thoughts weren't really with him. Something Bill Ryder had said about the rapes was hovering at the edge of her mind, just beyond the level at which her consciousness could retrieve it. She was trying to hook it in . . .

The car was now speeding through the outer suburbs. Jimmy, having finally finished his lunch, spoke with clear articulation for the first time:

'Sidcup. Garden of Kent. Home of the Median Man.'

'Skip the Alan Whicker,' said Maggie, 'and just deliver me to Mr and Mrs Portman.'

This Jimmy did, path-finding his way through Sidcup as though he'd lived in the area all his life, although he'd never been there before.

Maggie often marvelled at this facility of her sergeant, not quite appreciating how much advance preparation went into it all and what a photographic memory he had for maps.

They rolled up outside the Portmans' house with Jimmy's usual precision. Like Maggie's, it was semi-detached, but larger and more solid, set further back from the road behind a privet hedge and quite a large area of lawn, with a pathway of golden gravel leading around from the gate to the front door.

It was well-maintained and painted. It spoke somehow of thrift and careful planning and sensibleness.

They walked up the drive, noting the discreetly opaque nylon drapes at each window, and rang the bell. The door was opened by a small, mild-looking man in strongly magnifying spectacles.

He looked like henpecking timber, but, at the same

time, there was a hint of some considerable strength of character underneath.

'I'm sorry,' he said, straight away, 'we don't want anything and we'd rather not be bothered by anyone just now.'

The softness came into Maggie's face as she saw the suffering in his. All she needed was this man's face to confirm their supposition that the Portmans were Melody's parents:

'I'm Detective Inspector Forbes,' she said, showing her card, 'and this is Detective Sergeant Fenton. There's something we'd like to talk to you about. Perhaps you can guess what it is. I take it that you are Mr Gerald Portman.'

She saw his shoulders sag and an expression of resignation creep into his face. His innate toughness showed itself, however, in his refusal to commit himself instantly in words; 'Won't you come in?' he said, simply.

He led them into the living room, which was airy and pleasant, traditionally furnished – 'Times Furnishing' with a touch of 'Maple's' Maggie would have guessed. There were two beautiful yellow begonias on either side of the French windows to the garden.

Staring, unseeing, out into the garden was a thickening, large-boned woman, whom Maggie took to be Agatha Portman, Gerald Portman's wife.

She turned around as they came in. Maggie could see that she had been crying.

'Dear,' said Gerald Portman, 'this is Detective Inspector Forbes and Detective Sergeant Fenton – '

Fear leaped darkly into Agatha Portman's eyes: 'What do they want here? We've got nothing to do with the police. What do they want with us?'

She clenched her hands in front of her, knuckles white with tension.

Despite her big-boned, battleaxe image, there was a vulnerability about her which touched Maggie.

'We think you might be able to help us on an enquiry,' she said, carefully. 'A girl was killed last night – '

'We don't know anything about that, we don't know about any girl!' Mrs Portman exclaimed.

'She called herself Melody,' said Jimmy.

'We don't know anybody called Melody,' said Mrs Portman.

'How about Julia Portman, then?' asked Maggie, gently.

Mrs Portman became agitated, pacing about, wrenching at curtains that were already hanging impeccably: 'No, no – we don't know any Julia Portman, either!'

She turned her head away and took out a handkerchief from her sleeve.

There was a pause.

Then Gerald Portman spoke quietly, compassionate eyes large behind his spectacles, looking at his wife's wide, defenceless back:

'Julia Portman was our daughter,' he admitted, quietly. 'She . . . she called herself Melody.'

Mrs Portman whirled around, pink-nosed, watery-eyed: 'She didn't! She didn't!' she cried wildly. 'We don't know anyone called Melody!'

Portman moved to her quickly, put a protective arm around her. This fellow might look a bit mousey, but he was a man all right, thought Jimmy. Certainly, against all appearances, he was the stronger of this pair:

'Come on, love,' Portman told his wife, 'it's no use. I did warn you.'

He turned to Maggie and Jimmy, his arm still around his wife: 'When we saw it in the papers this morning – the name Melody and that address, we knew it was Julia. I wanted to ring the police and tell them, but

Agatha was against it. She got in a terrible state. I couldn't blame her, but I told her you'd easily find out who the girl really was, anyway.'

'It wasn't that easy, Mr Portman,' said Maggie.

'If we hadn't found an envelope addressed to her – ' added Jimmy.

'There! You see?' Agatha Portman burst out to her husband. 'I told you not to write to her! I told you to stop writing to her! Now look where it's landed us!'

She pulled herself free from her husband's protective arm.

He looked apologetically, on behalf, as it were, of his wife, at Maggie and Jimmy.

Maggie addressed herself quietly to her, persuasively: 'We'd have found out eventually, Mrs Portman. We always do. It would have taken longer, that's all. And the waiting would only have made it worse for you.'

She moved closer to Mrs Portman, tried to will her to raise her head and look at her: 'And in any case,' she went on, 'surely . . . surely you wouldn't want to disown your daughter . . . your own daughter, even if perhaps you disapproved of her. We want to find her killer. You must want that, too, don't you?'

'It wasn't true about her!' said Agatha Portman. She wandered about the room, wrenching at her handkerchief, addressing her remarks this way and that, never directly to any of the other people in the room: 'All those disgusting things they implied about her in the newspapers!'

She suddenly became distraught again, rounding on her husband: 'We'll have to move away from here, you know! We can't go on living here after this!'

'Mrs Portman, there's no need for that,' Maggie told her, reassuringly. She never ceased to marvel how scandal was often the uppermost worry in people's minds at times like this. Maybe it was a mental reflex to prevent themselves thinking about the much greater pain underneath. 'By the time we've caught the killer,' she continued, 'and he's been brought to trial, the Press will have lost interest. Tell me, did you see your daughter regularly?'

Mrs Portman continued to pace, talking more to herself than to anyone else:

'She was a . . . hostess, that's what she was. Long evening gown, little evening bag, I daresay. Nothing wrong in that. There are some very respectable establishments in London these days.'

Maggie gave her up, for the moment, as a bad job and turned to her husband: 'Mr Portman?'

But Agatha Portman, in her sensible tweed skirt and brown cardigan, was not to be stopped: 'I dare say she had a nice little flat, too, though I never saw it,' she rambled on, 'smart little car of her own – '

'Mr Portman?' Maggie asked again.

He was watching his wife, anxiously: 'Yes?' he asked, absently.

'I was asking you if either of you saw your daughter regularly.'

He pulled his concentration together: 'Yes . . . yes . . . I've seen her quite a few times since she . . . moved . . . to the . . . West End, yes. My wife wouldn't, but I thought, well . . . family, you know.'

'I know,' said Maggie.

'I'm an assistant bank manager, you see,' he went on, encouraged by Maggie's sympathetic smile, 'and sometimes I have to go up to Head Office in the City. Julia and I would meet for lunch. She always looked very smart, I will say that. Always a good handbag and always good shoes. They say you can tell a woman by her handbag and her shoes, don't they?'

'D'you happen to know what size she took?' asked Maggie. 'Was it a six?'

'No, those weren't hers,' said Agatha Portman, 'she was an eight D.'

'Did she ever mention any of her . . . er . . . associates?' asked Jimmy. 'A man called Miller, for instance?'

'No,' said Mr Portman, 'she hardly mentioned men at all.'

Jimmy followed it up, harder than Maggie. This was the way they played the game: 'What did she say she did for a living?' he enquired, blank-faced.

'I didn't ask,' answered Portman.

'You didn't ask?' said Jimmy, a note of incredulity in his voice. 'Weren't you interested?'

'No,' said Portman. 'It was enough just to see her and talk to her.'

'But you must have wondered,' Jimmy persisted. 'You must have asked yourself where all those "good shoes" and "good handbags" were coming from.'

Mrs Portman suddenly intervened hysterically as Maggie, who had been watching her closely, had been afraid she would: 'How dare you!' she cried. 'If you're implying! . . . There's such a thing as slander, you know. I know the police – they're as bad as the newspapers.'

She turned to Maggie: 'Are you going to allow your sergeant to stand there insulting our dead daughter with these vile innuendoes?'

'Mrs Portman, we don't like this any more than you do,' said Maggie, gently. 'We're just trying to get at the truth. My sergeant isn't trying to be hurtful and he's not trying to slander your daughter. Why should he? He didn't even know her. You must understand that this is all just routine to us, our everyday job. We make no judgements and we don't criticise.'

'I'd like to see you go through it and be so detached,' accused Mrs Portman.

She'd gone through it, thought Maggie, when her husband had been killed. She'd gone through it all right. She was still going through it, in a way . . . Hastily, she switched her thoughts back to the job. She turned to Gerald Portman, tactfully nudging him back to the track on to which Jimmy had got him:

'Mr Portman? . . . Your daughter's good living?'

He cast an apologetic glance at his wife: 'Well, I did think she might have a rich boy-friend or something . . . but she was a grown-up woman, it was her own business.' His voice became emphatic: 'But I had no idea she was a . . . I still don't think she was. I think there's been some terrible mix-up. I think it'll all be sorted out and then you'll see.'

'Oh, come on, Mr Portman,' said Jimmy, sustaining his role as the hard man, 'there must have been some signs in her flat.'

'I'd never been there,' said Portman. 'She always insisted we met wherever we were lunching.'

'When did you last see her, Mr Portman?' asked Maggie.

'About a month ago. We had lunch at a little restaurant just off Knightsbridge.'

'Can you remember the name of the restaurant?'

'Er, yes, it was called "La Lune Blanche".'

'And she didn't mention any trouble – with this . . . boy-friend, for instance.'

'No, she seemed in very good spirits,' said Portman.

'Did she say why?' Jimmy butted in. 'I mean why she was in such a good mood.'

'No,' said her father, nostalgically trying to recapture the essence of the lighthearted girl whom he'd lost, in a sense, twice, 'she always was one for a laugh and looking on the bright side of things.'

'I see,' concluded Maggie. 'Thank you for being so helpful. I know how difficult it must be for you.'

She hesitated: this was often the hardest part of all. It had been . . . for her:

'If you'd just come with us,' she added, 'we'll have to ask you to identify the . . . body . . . formally. Then we'll take a statement.'

Mrs Portman shrieked, as Maggie knew she would. Her husband put his arm round her again and she buried her sobbing face in his shoulder.

'You'll only need one of us, won't you?' asked Mr Portman.

'Yes.'

'Give me two minutes,' he said, 'then I'll be with you.'

Maggie took the hint and they went outside to the hall. They heard Portman murmuring to his wife as to an inconsolable child. They did not look at each other.

That night, Maggie was in her living room with George and Steve.

Steve was in the corner watching some American cops and robbers rubbish on television. One of the heroes was wearing jeans so tight he was bound to be sterile before he was thirty. George was reading his newspaper.

Maggie had Steve's monk's costume on her electric sewing machine and was speaking her thoughts aloud, sorting out her day:

'I wouldn't mind,' she said, 'but Croft has changed the whole balance, you know what I mean, Dad? Now Miller's got the initiative. If I try to lean on him again, he can claim harrassment.'

She turned to Steve: 'Will you turn that thing down! I won't ask you again!'

Steve reached over amiably enough and turned down the volume.

'And come over here a sec, would you,' added Maggie.

'Can't I wait 'til the end of this?' asked Steve, plaintively.

'Not if you want this habit in time,' said Maggie.

'Then I think I'll kick the habit,' said Steve.

Maggie and George groaned in unison. Steve dragged himself reluctantly from the TV and came over to Maggie.

His eyes lit up:

'Wow! It's looking really good!'

'Here, just slip it on,' said Maggie.

Steve slipped it over his head and started dragging away towards the mirror:

'Let's have a butcher's?' he asked.

'Hold on!' shouted Maggie, who was still attached to it.

She filled her mouth with pins and let Steve drag her over to the mirror.

She pulled up a chair, put a newspaper on it and spoke with her mouth full of pins:

'Here, stand on this.'

Having him up on the chair made it easier for her to make the final adjustments and pinnings to the hem without kneeling down.

'Right on!' said Steve, admiring as much as he could see of himself in the mirror from his elevated position. 'How do I look, granddad?'

'Like a nasturtium,' said George.

'You mean a Cistercian,' said Steve.

'You mean what you mean and I'll mean what I mean,' answered George, without taking his eyes off the paper.

Steve struck a pulpit-like pose and assumed a voice which he believed to be like that of a vicar:

'My dear flock, whom I have so often fleeced,' he intoned.

'Hold still or I'll fleece you,' said Maggie. She started pinning up the hem.

After having Portman identify his daughter's body, one of the jobs she always dreaded, she had left Jimmy to get down his statement, gone to visit the latest rape victim, Susan Ross, in the hospital, to see if she might have remembered any more details about her victim – she hadn't – she had come home; only an hour late for a change.

There had been no point in hanging around. She admitted to herself that she needed a break on the murder case. She needed someone to turn up Ruby. For some reason, she was turning more and more to the hunch that the redhead held the key to Melody's murder.

On the rape case an idea was slowly forming in her mind. It was forming slowly, in the twilight, as so many of her best ideas did. But this one she was reluctant to let out into the full light of day. She was afraid of it. She was glad to be able to immerse herself in domesticity for a change, just like any other woman.

George read out a bit from the paper, a habit of which he was fond. If he got to a paper first, you were lucky to read anthing in it you hadn't already heard about by the time he'd let it go.

'It says here,' he announced, 'that ninety per cent of murders that aren't solved in the first twenty-four hours aren't solved at all.'

'That was America,' said Steve.

Maggie, pins in her mouth, concentrating on the hem, said grimly: 'That's not going to happen here, not in this case.'

Unlike a lot of policemen, she enjoyed talking over her cases with her family. Maybe it was a habit she had got into with her husband, both being in the same job, but she thought it had more to do with the often refreshing difference of the non-professional point of view. It often threw a light from the side, as it were, which her trained mind either hadn't seen, or had seen and ignored.

'I don't see where you've got to go on it,' George commented.

'I've got Ruby,' she said, 'and I've got the fact that someone *must* have seen something – a man looking distraught or running away, even someone with blood on him. I've got the night-shift going through Mayfair like a vacuum cleaner.'

In the event, it wasn't Maggie's famous vacuum cleaner that came up with the goods. It was a small police force on the south coast.

Just as Maggie had got halfway round the hem on Steve's robe, the telephone rang.

It was the desk sergeant. 'We've got "Red" Ruby here, ma'am,' he told her. 'They picked her up down at Dover.'

She went back into the living room, shrugging into a short jacket:

'We've got something,' she said, urgently. 'Take over, will you, Dad?'

She handed him a handful of pins. 'Goodnight, Steve, love. Goodnight, Dad.'

'But, Mum – ' said Steve.

But she was gone.

George advanced menacingly on Steve, a heap of pins in his hand.

'Now, granddad,' said Steve, nervously.

'You'd better keep still, my son,' said George, grinning hugely, 'my bins ain't what they were.'

In the car on her way into town, Maggie picked up the telephone, then put it down again. She hadn't the heart to hook Jimmy out again. She knew he had another heavy date, of which he had great hopes. If she kept on frustrating him, she'd end up with a neurotic, unstable sergeant on her hands – which started her thinking about the rapist again. But she didn't want to think of him just now. To be honest, she'd prefer not to think of him again, ever.

But she was going to have to.

She prayed that Ruby would have the answers she needed. Once she'd got Melody's murder out of the way, perhaps she could face what had to be done about the bastard who ruined girl's lives without killing them.

If she didn't catch him soon there was the distinct possibility that he would start killing them as well. Bill Ryder had said the man was getting more violent with each attack.

She reached the station in record time, swept in to the desk sergeant:

'Where is she?' she asked.

'Interview Room Two, ma'am,' he said.

'Send a couple of cups of tea in, would you, sergeant?' she asked.

'Right away, ma'am.'

'Oh, and a packet of cigarettes. I take it Ruby still smokes?'

'Like a chimney, ma'am.'

Maggie went into Room Two. Ruby was just stubbing out her last fag in the ashtray, which was half full of her lipsticked dog-ends, and having no luck extracting another one from the somewhat po-faced uniformed WPC who was with her.

She was in a very nervous state and therefore disposed to be aggressive:

'Here, what is all this?' she hit Maggie with as she entered. 'This ain't Russia, you know. The citizenry is allowed to come and go as it bleeding pleases.'

Unlike the other girls, she was as Cockney as a winkle-seller at Aldgate on a Sunday morning.

'Funny you should say that,' answered Maggie. 'I

was just thinking – why Dover? Thinking of skipping the country, Rube?'

'I ain't saying nothing,' said Ruby, 'until my solicitor gets here.'

'Oh, come on, Ruby,' said Maggie. 'You know and I know that you haven't got a solicitor, so why mess about?'

If she'd wanted a solicitor, Maggie had to admit to herself, all Ruby would have to do would be to crook her little finger in the direction of one. She was a stunning looking girl with a mop of red hair and emerald eyes and a fantastic pair of legs, which were sheathed at the moment in spotted tights and a skirt like an eye-shade.

A young constable came in with the tea and a fresh pack of Benson and Hedges. He nearly missed the table completely with the tray in his engrossment with eyeing Ruby.

This was good for Ruby's morale. As was the tea. As were the cigarettes. She started, Maggie noted, to relax a little.

'Why Dover, Ruby?' she repeated. 'Were you really thinking of skipping the country?'

''Course not,' said Ruby, with a look indicating that an old mate should know better. 'I was going to work the cross-Channel ferries for a bit, wasn't I? – Give the punters their duty-frees.'

'You weren't running away or anything?' asked Maggie, swiftly.

Ruby was lighting a cigarette from the new pack.

'Running away?' As the cigarette glowed, the full significance of Maggie's question hit her: 'Here! You don't think I – '

'Did you?'

'Oh, do leave off!' said Ruby.

'Then why did you run?' Maggie insisted.

'I didn't run!' said Ruby, exasperated. 'I *told* you – I just fancied a change.'

'Just like that.'

'Just like bloody that!'

Maggie let a pause develop while she sipped her tea. Defiantly, Ruby sipped hers, too, blew an insouciant cloud of smoke up at the ceiling.

'Any ideas who did top Melody?' Maggie asked, suddenly. 'After all, you must have seen a lot of her regulars.'

'How d'you reckon that, then?'

Maggie rose abruptly: 'I want you to come with me.'

She nodded to the uniformed WPC, who opened the door: 'Would you like a sergeant from CID, ma'am?' she asked.

'No, thank you, Prenn,' Maggie smiled. 'Ruby and I are old friends.'

'Here,' said Ruby, mentally dragging her feet, 'where we going? Where you taking me, then? I don't want to – '

Maggie smiled sweetly: 'Just shut it and come on,' she said – 'old friend!'

They sped smoothly through the West End. The theatres had long since let out the cinemas and the streets were comparatively free. Free, that is, by London standards. A provincial city might have considered itself in the grip of a late night traffic jam.

They speared through Soho, Ruby mentally comparing herself to the blown-up photographs of the girls outside the strip clubs and feeling justifiably smug about the comparison.

The exercise helped her to combat the war of nerves Maggie was waging on her. From the minute they had got into the car, Maggie had not uttered a word, apart from an injunction to her not to smoke: 'I don't like smoking in my car,' she said. And Ruby knew that was part of the psychological campaign as well. Maggie knew that being denied a fag always made her nervous.

They drew up outside Melody's block of flats. Ruby turned and stared at Maggie's profile.

'All right,' said Maggie. 'Out.'

'Maggie – ' said Ruby.

Maggie indicated the flats entrance. 'In,' she said.

Ruby undulated obediently across the pavement at Maggie's side like a well-behaved, but precociously well-developed child:

'Come on, Mags, what's on?' she pleaded.

'Time enough,' answered Maggie mercilessly. 'You'll see.'

They went into the luxurious lobby of the now sinister-seeming apartment block.

They rode up in the lift, froze off the tentative advances of a mildly inebriated out-of-towner, who had heard about the reputation of the block and thought he'd got lucky, and were let into Melody's flat by the police constable who was still on guard outside the door.

Inside Maggie paused, deliberately, as if to look at her hair in a mirror just inside the living room as they came through the small vestibule.

Ruby stared, her eyes stricken, at the bloodstains still on the wall and now rapidly darkening. Remembering Melody, as she did, full of life and exuberance, they seemed especially obscene.

Maggie, apparently preoccupied with her hair, watched the other girl closely:

'Funny to think,' she said, casually, 'that a couple of nights ago she was here . . . fine . . . happy with the world . . . no worries. Just like you.'

Ruby seemed unable to tear her eyes away from the bloodstains: 'Yeah . . .' she said.

'It's the little things that get me,' said Maggie. She

crossed the living room: 'Like . . . she hadn't had time to plump up the cushions on the sofa. Look . . . see?'

She pointed out the indentations where someone had sat.

Ruby came over to her reluctantly: 'Yeah . . .' she said.

Maggie went into the bedroom: 'Then there's her clothes,' she said. 'Have a butcher's in here.' Her eyes compelled Ruby to join her. She went into the walk-in wardrobe: 'I mean, what's going to happen to all this lot? Lovely stuff.'

A pair of shoes came flying out to land just in front of Ruby:

'And all these shoes!' Maggie went on. 'Hardly worn.'

More shoes came flying out, followed by Maggie.

'They'd do you a treat, Rube,' she said. 'Try one on.'

She handed Ruby one of the shoes – an eight: 'Go on,' she urged, 'try it and see.'

Reluctantly, Ruby put it on. It swamped her, a large gap showing between her heel and the back of the shoe.

'Oh dear,' said Maggie. 'Never mind – try this one.'

She handed Ruby another shoe. Again Ruby was slow to slide into it. 'Come on, Rube, don't hang about!' said Maggie.

Ruby slid it on and this time it fitted perfectly. 'There we are – fits perfectly,' she said: 'that's a six; the first one was an eight. You always did have little feet for a tall girl, Rube.'

She picked up Ruby's own shoes, which she had removed to try the others on: 'Ooh, look!' she exclaimed, innocently: 'It's the same make, same size . . . everything.'

She held the shoes from the wardrobe and Ruby's own shoes together side by side.

She stared steadily at Ruby. 'Cinderella,' she said.

Ruby hesitated a fraction of a second and then spilled it:

'All right, all right!' she declared. 'So I *shared* with Melody.'

She started to pace about the lush carpet: 'Call girls – the punters are looking for class; not some old tom they pick up off the street. Once they've *seen* me . . . well, I've never had no one walk away. But over the 'phone – well, listen to me: I'm a right Cockney and we can't all fly in from Luton Airport! It's male chauvinistic sexual bloody snobbery, that's what it is! So Melody used to take my calls, make like she was me. As I said . . . once they got here and saw me . . .'

Ruby was beginning to shiver slightly. Maggie knew she had broken through. She was not going to push it just yet: 'Let's have a cup of tea, Rube,' she suggested, gently.

'I'll make it,' said Ruby.

'No, it's all right,' answered Maggie, making her way towards the tiny kitchen.

'No, come on,' said Ruby, 'I'll do it. After all, I know where everything is, don't I?' She got out the little china teapot, took the tea bags from a packet in a cupboard, filled and switched on the electric kettle.

Five minutes later they were sitting on one of the lemon sofas and Ruby was giving Maggie the rest of it:

'Look,' she started, 'one girl on her tod; okay. Two girls sharing – a brothel. Right? We get done – right? Well . . . I was coming back night before last, saw the law swarming all over the place, didn't want to take no chances, did I? So I turned round, dead casual and beat it. I had a quick drink at the "Fenwick" and caught the first train to Dover. Understand?'

'Yes,' replied Maggie. She never ceased to marvel at the kind of instant lives these girls led, the instant decisions they made, the lack of reflection.

Ruby was watching her as she lifted her cup to her lips:

'Well?' she asked Maggie.

Maggie studied her. Ruby had been frank with her. There was no reason to keep up the pressure: 'Ruby,' she said, 'if you help me I think I can promise to get a touch of amnesia about the brothel bit. Okay?'

Ruby finally relaxed completely: 'Okay.'

'Right,' said Maggie. 'Her regulars. Anyone strike you as odd?'

'No,' said Ruby. She reflected. 'Wait a minute, though. Yeah! There was one. Used to call on Melody about once a month or so. Dead out of place. Not the type.'

'Didn't know there was a type,' said Maggie.

'You're right in one way,' admitted Ruby. 'But on the game you get a kind of sixth sense. About who wants it and who don't: know what I mean? Well, I always got the feeling this punter didn't.'

'Maybe he was a talker.'

'Yeah, I thought of that. But there was something else funny as well.'

'Oh?' As always, Maggie's 'oh?' was heavy with invitations to confidences.

'Yeah,' Ruby went on. 'He always had some kind of parcel with him.'

'Parcel?'

'Or box,' said Ruby. 'About this big.' She demonstrated. 'I couldn't make it out. I mean, punters have their funny little ways, I know, but it beat me what could have been in this box every time. It was like that French movie – remember? Where this Japanese punter brings a box with him every time and you never see what's in it. Nearly drove me mad, that did. I mean – '

'Get on with it, Ruby,' Maggie broke in.

'Yeah, well,' said Ruby, 'one day I finally got a squint what was inside this geezer's box.'

Maggie put down her cup and leaned forward, fascinated: 'What was it?'

Ruby beamed triumphantly: 'A plant in a pot!' she said.

'A plant!'

'Yeah!' said Ruby. She looked around the room, saw the crimson begonia, now wilting a little because no one had thought to water it. 'Here, that must be one of them, I should think.'

Maggie's face went blank and Ruby mistook the expression for one of disappointment: she tailed off rather lamely, feeling that what she'd had to say hadn't added up to much after all. 'Well . . . it was just him not being the type and then the parcel every time and then it turning out to be a pot plant . . . Anyway,' she ended defensively.

Maggie leaned forward intently: 'Ruby; can you describe this man?'

'That's just it. I can't, really,' Ruby apologised. 'He was . . . sort of . . . nondescript. He'd be hard to pick out in a crowd.'

'That's just what I'd hoped you'd say,' said Maggie.

'You did?' Ruby was baffled.

'Thanks, Ruby, you've been a great help. I'd like you to come down to the station and put it all in a statement, if you would.'

'Yeah, 'course I will. Anything to catch the bastard who done Melody.' She looked a little embarrassed: 'And d'you think you could let me know when the funeral's going to be. I'd like to come – and I know all the other girls would, too.'

'I'll do that,' said Maggie. 'Now if you'll just hold on a tick, I've got a phone call to make, then we'll go down to the station.'

She crossed to the telephone. Ruby took the cups and saucers out to the kitchen. Maggie could hear her swilling them as she dialled:

'Give me Fingerprints,' said Maggie.

She gazed at the begonia. Her face was unaccountably sad.

She took Ruby to Seven Dials, left her with a constable on the night-shift to give her statement, had another brief word with Fingerprints, confirming what she wanted first thing in the morning, then drove home.

As she turned into her little garage space, her car clock showed 2.45.

She put on the lights in the living room on her way through to the kitchen to get a glass of water. All she wanted was to take an aspirin and sack out. Her eye fell on Steve's still unfinished costume, lying across the sewing machine.

Quietly, she closed the living room door, sat down at the machine, rubbed her eyes and started to sew . . .

Only the discipline of years saved her from oversleeping next morning. As it was, she rolled out of bed like some half-animated plastic doll and moved, automaton-like, to the bathroom.

She plunged into a cold shower, slipped into her jeans and sweater, knocked on Steve's door, then went downstairs and made a pot of thick, black coffee.

By the time she'd had three cups, her fatigue had started to roll away and her brain was gradually beginning to spark. She was pretty sure that today she was going to move in on Melody's murderer.

Steve came in, wearing the now completed robe, which he'd found on his way through the living room.

He gave Maggie a big kiss:

'It's neat, Mum! It's really neat!' he said. 'I'll bet old Abelard himself didn't have threads like these.'

'Turn round,' she said.

He twirled exaggeratedly.

'You'll do,' she said. 'Know your lines?'

'Yeah, most of them. Want to hear some? – '

'No, no ta,' said Maggie hastily, as he drew in a deep breath, 'haven't got the time, love. Got a couple of heavy assignments.'

She drained her last cup of coffee preparatory to leaving.

'You haven't even had any toast,' said Steve, accusingly.

'I'll have something in the canteen when I get to the station,' she promised. 'When your granddad comes, ask him to get a sliced brown loaf today – one of the big ones. 'Bye, love!'

She gave him a quick kiss and was gone.

Steve stood momentarily, then went to the cupboards and got out the cereal and a bowl. The house felt suddenly very empty. He switched on his radio. At least it was something . . .

A lorry had overturned on the Hammersmith flyover, causing a two mile tailback even at that time in the morning. Maggie finally got to Seven Dials with her blood hot and her temper short.

She strode through the CID room, barely acknowledging the ''Morning, ma'ams' and ''Morning, Inspectors', leaving a trail of expressive glances being exchanged behind her.

She swept into her office, looked for what she'd requested from Fingerprints the night before, didn't see it and snatched up the 'phone.

'Fingerprints,' she said, tartly.

As she said it, Jimmy came into the office with a clutch of blown-up photographs: ''Morning, chief; these what you're after?' he asked.

'Yes, they are what I'm after,' Maggie snapped, slamming down the telephone and snatching them from him. 'What are you doing with them?'

'Well, I found them here when I got in, didn't know what they were all about, so I took 'em down to Fingerprints to get 'em to explain them to me,' he said, apologetically. He could see the storm signals; it was a time for treading on eggshells.

'Sergeant, when I'm ready to let you take over my chair, I'll let you know,' she told him.

'Yes, chief,' he said, submissively, not really daunted, but understanding her and without resentment.

She really was a bitch, she thought to herself. She should be praising the kid for enthusiasm and initiative and here she was, bawling him out instead. 'Oh, hell, I'm sorry, Jimmy!' she exploded. 'It's just one of those mornings.'

''S'all right, chief, I know what you mean,' he said, with the ghost of a grin, 'I gave Fingerprints a bit of a mouthful myself when they couldn't exactly tell me what these were all about.'

In explanation, Maggie spread out the pictures on her desk:

'There were only two sets of prints on the plant pot with the begonia in it in Melody's flat. One set belonged to her. The other set is unidentified.'

'Yeah, I see,' said Jimmy, 'but I don't understand where it gets us.'

'What you don't know,' explained Maggie, 'is that they brought Ruby in last night. She told me Melody had a regular visitor, who always brought her a plant in a pot, a begonia. Now where have we seen some more of those just lately?'

It dawned on Jimmy's face almost immediately.

*

The bank where Gerald Portman worked was in the High Street. Its neat façade blended perfectly with the quiet trimness and order of British suburbia at its best. Murder, violence, blooded weapons and blood-splashed walls were the last things one would have associated with anyone having his being in this sort of environment. But Maggie knew from long experience that murder could breed anywhere and as she went into the bank she forced herself to remember that.

Gerald Portman was not there. 'He rang up this morning to say that he wasn't feeling well and that he wouldn't be in,' said the girl teller to whom Maggie had spoken, 'is there anyone else who can help you?'

'No, thank you,' said Maggie, who had gone in incognito, 'I'll call him tomorrow.'

She hurried out and jumped back into the car. 'He's not there,' she said, urgently. 'Round to his house and if you care to break any speed limits, feel free.'

Jimmy didn't need it in writing. He drove with polished speed through the heart of the town and out into the leafy outskirts where the Portmans lived.

Maggie sat, apparently still, but in reality fidgeting imperceptibly in every muscle. It was possible that they had let this one slip right through their fingers.

Jimmy swung the car up the drive of the Portmans' house and stopped outside the immaculate front door. Maggie and Jimmy climbed out. Jimmy rang the bell. There was no reply.

He rang again, louder this time. Still the house remained silent. Nobody came:

Maggie and Jimmy looked at each other, then went around the side of the house. They tried the door leading to the back garden. It was unlocked.

They went through into the garden. It was impeccably groomed, the lawn shaved to a flawless green velvet, the borders ablaze with colour.

Abutting on to the house was a large greenhouse.

In the greenhouse, in a gardener's apron and gloves, was Gerald Portman. He was busily potting a begonia.

The greenhouse, like the garden, was a riot of colour, with dozens of flowering shrubs waiting to be planted out.

The whole scene was almost a caricature of the skilled, obsessive English amateur gardener at his hobby.

Maggie and Jimmy went cautiously into the greenhouse.

Portman did not even look up. He simply carried on calmly with what he was doing, caring fingers pressing and dabbing the soil around the bright red begonia. His whole manner was of the total tranquillity of someone who has passed through great pain into serenity. It was almost as if he were out of their reach.

Maggie spoke first: 'We went to the bank, but they said you hadn't been in.'

Portman still didn't look up: 'No,' he said, 'I decided to take the day off. I didn't want it to happen at the bank.'

'Where's your wife?' asked Jimmy.

'She's out shopping,' said Portman. 'It's her day for the big shopping.'

'You know why we're here, Mr Portman, don't you,' said Maggie. 'We want to talk to you again.'

For the first time, he looked up at them, pale blue eyes big and inoffensive behind the magnifying lenses: 'Yes, I understand,' he said, calmly.

'Why don't we go into the house?' Maggie suggested.

It was as if he hadn't heard her. He started to talk, mildly, but earnestly, as if anxious to make them understand:

'It had to be done, you see,' he explained. 'She had a

good upbringing. Godfearing upbringing. But . . . somehow . . . it didn't take.' He looked at them interestedly, trying to find the parallel. 'You know – the way a vaccination sometimes doesn't take. Yes, that's . . . that's the nearest I can get to it. It started with boys at school. Then older men; she found there was money to be made with them. She . . . liked . . . it in any case, but she found there was money to be made, too. When she left school I got her a job with the bank. But she only stayed a few days. She said she could make more in an hour than she got in a week at the bank – and it was more fun. That's what she said . . . it was more fun. She didn't seem to think about . . . it . . . the way we do.'

He turned back to his potting and was silent for a few seconds before going on. When he continued, his voice was as mild as ever:

'I used to go and see her at that place of hers . . . I used to reason with her. I always' – he gestured around the greenhouse – 'always took her a plant.'

He paused and wiped his forehead with the back of his glove, leaving a dirty smudge.

'I tried to show her how . . . clean and . . . sweet they were. I could tell she was getting more and more fed up with me. She told me not to come again – ever.'

He paused again, then spoke very simply, almost like a child: 'She had to be killed,' he concluded, looking from one to the other as if they would understand.

Maggie and Jimmy exchanged a glance. There was compassion in it for Portman.

Portman turned away, picked up the plant he had been potting. He handed it to Maggie: 'Here, this is for you,' he said. 'I know you don't have a lot to brighten up those police offices of yours.'

'Thank you,' said Maggie. She took the plant very gently. 'Shall we go?' she asked.

They took him back to Seven Dials and while Jimmy

took him to Interview Room One to get his statement, Maggie went to report to Detective Chief Inspector Russell.

Croft was with him. Maggie wished he hadn't been. Something, she knew, was going to come up which would be embarrassing.

'You mean he coughed?' asked Russell. 'The whole thing? Just like that?'

'Just like that,' said Maggie.

'Well done!' said Russell. Croft remained straight-faced and silent.

'You cautioned him first, of course,' added Russell.

It was the question Maggie knew would come and had been dreading:

'No, there wasn't a chance – '

'Wasn't a chance?' Insofar as the rugged face ever expressed anything, it now expressed incredulity: 'Then the whole thing's not worth a piece of wet string! You know it's not admissible as evidence if he wasn't cautioned!'

She didn't look at Croft, but she could swear she could *feel* him smirking. Of course she knew it wasn't admissible as evidence. Christ, what did Bill Russell take her for, a bloody rookie?

She swallowed her temper and answered evenly: 'No, I know that, sir, but it just poured out of him. I don't think he'd have even heard a caution if we'd given him one.'

'And what if he's had second thoughts, takes it all back now he sees a nick closing in on him? It has been known, you know,' Russell pointed out, his voice as dry as an egg-timer.

'I don't think he'll do that, sir; you haven't met him. He needs to confess.'

'Then I suggest you get along and keep that need on the boil, Inspector. If he goes cold, you're in trouble.'

'Yes, sir.'

She went out, her cheeks burning, and made her way to the interview room, praying that Portman hadn't had second thoughts.

He hadn't. He was in exactly the same frame of mind as he had been in the greenhouse and on the ride into town.

Jimmy was with him and a detective constable was just finishing taking down his statement.

'You did caution him?' asked Maggie, anxiously.

Jimmy gave her a 'do me a favour!' sort of look, or as close to one as he dared, but said, merely: 'Yes, Inspector.'

She knew he would have done, but nevertheless breathed a silent sigh of relief. That was that wrapped up.

She went to her office, rifled through the pile of case files, which never seemed to get any less.

She called in four detective sergeants to get their current reports.

She wanted to clear her mind now to focus on the rape case. She had never stopped thinking about it all the time she was on the murder, but now she wanted to crystallise the thoughts that had been gradually cohering in the back of her mind.

The telephone rang. It was Ruby: 'You haven't forgotten Melody's funeral, Maggie? Three o'clock this afternoon I was just told.' Damn! She had forgotten.

'No, Ruby,' she said, 'I hadn't forgotten.'

'Only the girls would . . . appreciate it . . . if you was there.'

It was strange, the relationship between Maggie and the girls on her patch. She knew them all, not only the high-flyers, the call girls, but the toms as well, the girls who prowled the streets. She knew them all and they knew her. She didn't agree with much of the law on prostitution, but she administered as fairly and dispassionately as she could. The girls respected her, admired her, even – some of them – felt a certain wistful envy of her.

'I'll be there, Ruby,' she promised. Three o'clock. Give it half an hour. Steve's school play was at four-fifteen. She could just make it . . .

They stood around Melody's grave as the coffin was lowered in, Ruby, Margot, Letty, Charlie, Georgia, Annabelle and Pauline. They were all in discreetly elegant black, looking like half a dozen beautiful, mourning heiresses.

All of them were in tears.

Maggie and Jimmy stood behind them in silence, a little distance away.

'Ashes to ashes and dust to dust . . .'

Maggie looked at the semi-circle of shapely legs around the grave, in their expensive footwear.

Letty was in a pair of glove leather, clinging boots that couldn't have cost less than two hundred quid, Charlie was in Gucci, Ruby's small feet were encased in . . . Ruby!!!

Maggie turned suddenly to Jimmy: 'We got it wrong!' she whispered, fiercely.

'We what?' Jimmy gazed at her, bewildered.

'Never mind! Come on!'

As quickly as they decently could, they backed away from the group around the grave and hurried to their car on the road at the edge of the cemetery.

Jimmy took off as if he were trying to make the moon.

Agatha Portman opened the door to them at the immaculate house in Sidcup. Her eyes were sore from weeping, but her large-boned face was composed. There were two packed suitcases in the hall.

She led them into the living room, an inner dignity informing her solid, matronly figure that hadn't been there when they had first met her:

'If you hadn't come, I was coming to you,' she said.

She stood there in the middle of the bright, suburban drawing room, the dazzling green of the lawn visible through the french windows, her fingers interlaced as if to hold on to her hard-won composure:

'I found I couldn't,' she said. 'I couldn't let him take the blame. It was his idea that he should. He talked me into it. Gerald has always been the decision-maker, you know. People underestimate him. They've always thought that I was the strong one, but it was Gerald.

'He argued that they'd be more lenient with him, looking so meek and mousy, than they would with me, looking . . . well, you can see how I look. And he said he'd get more sympathy than me on account of the father-daughter relationship. He said a lot of people always think there's some jealousy somewhere between mothers and daughters. Gerald can be very persuasive . . . very convincing.'

'Yes, he can,' agreed Maggie, with feeling, glancing at Jimmy.

Mrs Portman continued: 'I was to go off and live with my sister in Cheltenham, sell the house, cut all my connections with the district. He said it would be best for both of us, that he'd just wither away if I went to prison, but he could stand prison if he knew I was free. He convinced me at the time, but once he'd gone, I knew it wasn't right. I couldn't let him do it.'

She looked at Maggie with genuine curiosity: 'How did you . . . know?'

'It just hit me,' said Maggie, frankly. 'I suddenly remembered that, when we first talked, you denied that you'd ever been to your daughter's flat, yet you knew there were two different sizes of shoes there. "Those weren't hers", you said, when I asked if your daughter took a six.'

'You're very clever,' said Mrs Portman.

'Not that clever,' answered Maggie, ruefully, 'otherwise I'd have spotted it there and then.'

'How did it happen?' asked Jimmy, 'and I must caution you that anything you say may be used in evidence.'

'Oh, I don't care about that,' said Agatha Portman, 'I just want to get it over with now. It's all been a nightmare. It's been a nightmare for years, ever since she reached her teens.'

For the first time, her composure showed signs of cracking. She recovered it and went on:

'I went to plead with her once more that night. Oh, I'd done it often enough before, God knows! But this time she went wild. She flew at me; didn't even give me a chance to get my gloves off or my hat. She'd just been with a man; I saw him coming out. She had . . . nothing on . . . under her dressing gown. She said vile things . . . terrible . . . things I didn't even know about. Then she said she'd already had two abortions . . . two of God's creatures! I screamed at her!'

Mrs Portman's calm façade had been gradually cracking as she talked. Her face crumpled, tears started to trickle down her cheeks: 'Then I . . . I didn't really know I'd done it until I saw her lying there.'

The tears turned into sobs, great wrenching sobs wracking that big frame. And Maggie, almost without knowing it, found herself cradling the big woman, rocking her as if she were a child, saying nothing, judging nothing.

Jimmy looked on, quietly marvelling. Would he ever completely suss out this extraordinary guv'nor of his?

They took her back to Seven Dials where she was reunited with her husband. They clung to each other like passionate kids. Don't let anyone ever tell me, thought Maggie, that love dies when the fever in the blood cools down. That's what she and Bob would have still felt about each other at the Portmans' age if . . .

She shut the thought off instantly and went to explain to Russell.

She had expected a lot of flak from him. She got none: merely a cool appraisal of the situation: 'You sure they're not pulling the old double confession gag – trying to make it impossible to be certain which one did it?'

'Yes, sir, absolutely certain,' said Maggie. 'Portman's now admitted he was lying.'

'So we do him for obstruction of the police.'

'No, sir, I'd rather not.' It was easy for him, she thought. To him they were just names on a crime sheet; he wasn't involved. And that's exactly the argument he'd turn round against her if she used it. She shouldn't be involved, either. A copper had to be dispassionate, detached.

Guilefully, she found another answer to his querying eyebrows:

'It wouldn't look good,' she said. 'He's not a criminal. Just a man trying to protect his wife. They're just ordinary, decent people who've been through a terrible experience, a tragedy, together. They've got a lot more suffering coming to them; what's happened is going to be with them for the rest of their lives. If we went by the book on the false confession, I hate to think of the Press we'd get. And what the public would think of us.'

'Public Relations Officer, too, now, are you, Maggie?'

As soon as she heard the 'Maggie' she knew she was home and dry.

Russell's lips twitched imperceptibly. She was a crafty devil, this one. Quick brain. He liked that. It balanced the dangers created by that big heart. It also helped her to make the kind of deductive leap she had made that afternoon; from Gerald Portman to Agatha Portman: that was smart detective work:

'Very well,' he said, 'it's your case. You know I don't interfere.' Not interfere! thought Maggie. If he took it into his head, he'd interfere in a fight between two Bengal tigers.

It was as she left Russell's office that it hit her: Steve's play! She looked at her watch. Five to five. Oh, God! Maybe she could catch the last bit.

She grabbed Jimmy, told him to take over and raced for her car.

As she weaved her way through the beginning of the build-up of the rush hour she cursed police work, the police system, the nature of the human animal that made police necessary at all.

This was where being a copper took its toll – on one's human relationships, family life. You could never be sure of keeping a date. You daren't throw a dinner party.

You couldn't even keep your word about getting to see your son in his school play.

It was pushing five minutes to six when she finally sweated her way through to the school at Ealing. It was manifestly closed. The gates were locked.

Leaning against them as she screeched to a stop was Steve, looking sardonic, his monk's robe folded over his arm.

Maggie jumped out of the car and rushed over to him:

'Steve, love, I'm sorry! Oh, I'm sorry!'

He pushed himself off from the gates with the flat of his foot, which he had bent up against the gates in an attitude of bored resignation.

Slowly, as he studied Maggie's stricken face, a smile stole over his: 'You didn't miss much,' he said. 'As a matter of fact, I was absolutely bloody horrible!'

'Still,' said Maggie, 'I said I'd be there; and I'll bet you weren't lousy.'

They walked towards the car. She linked him. 'It wasn't that I forgot,' she said, 'it honestly wasn't. I just got tangled up in this murder and there was no way I could leave it.'

'Well,' he grinned, in a Western drawl, 'I guess a man's gotta do what a man's gotta do – even if he's a woman!'

She laughed as they got into the car. 'Tell you what,' she said, 'I'll thrash you in a game of tennis before dinner!'

'You'll what?' he asked, mockingly.

She drove home fast and they rushed in and upstairs to get their gear. George was in the kitchen – which he preferred to the living room – reading his imperishable paper.

'Hello, Dad!'

''Lo, granddad!'

'What was it like, then?' he shouted after them as they bolted past the door.

'Lousy!' shouted Steve.

'What? After all my Norman Hartnell?' he demanded.

Five minutes later, they were bolting down the stairs again; tennis gear on and rackets in their hands.

'It says here in the paper – ' he started. But they were gone and he heard the car starting up.

'Kids!' he said to himself, impartially as between the two of them. To him Maggie was just as much still a kid as Steve; just a slightly older one.

On the Municipal tennis courts Maggie, in her shirt and tennis shorts, was proving, as usual, a principal attraction. Her lithe, smoothly muscled body, kept at full stretch by Steve's positively vicious game, turned a number of other players on surrounding courts into spectators.

Steve was a natural ball player. Give him any game with a ball in it and his co-ordination and eye slid into mesh and he became a formidable opponent after just a couple of lessons. And he had had more than a couple of lessons at school.

Maggie, too, had been taught in her schooldays and she had a lot more experience than her son. And soon those who had stopped to watch her body, stayed to watch the play.

Steve didn't play down to her. He couldn't afford to. Once he started thinking of her as a woman or as his mother, to be treated gently, firstly she would be annoyed and secondly she would start beating the hell out of him.

So they went at it hammer and hell. Steve had a service like a kicking mule, but Maggie had raking, top-spin ground strokes. Serve, volley, smash, lob, the sweat pouring, the tensions of the day being hosed away by the adrenalin, the fine skin gently flushed underneath, Maggie was joyous. Not once did she think of work and not once, especially, did she ponder the idea that was creeping up on her about the rape case.

Steve ran out the winner, 3–6, 7–5, 7–5. 'Thanks, Bjorn,' said Maggie. 'Now what d'you say to a hamburger?'

'MacDonald's, you mean?' asked Steve, enthusiastically.

'No, one of mine,' said Maggie, twisting his ear.

'Oh . . .' he said.

'Well, thanks for the vote of confidence!' said Maggie.

They drove back home, deliciously tired, parried the sarcastic enquiries of George as to when they were turning pro, then Steve had hamburger, egg, chips, beans and fried tomatoes while Maggie and George got by on the hamburger and chips.

Then Steve and Maggie sat side by side watching TV while George read. During the commercials they talked about school, Steve's coming soccer match against Edgware Comprehensive, how he was coming along on his weak subject, Geography, and what a berk the History Master was.

Of girls they didn't speak, Steve being at a particularly sensitive stage in his relationships with them, one delicious little blonde in particular.

From time to time, George recited bits out of the paper to them: 'It's as good as having it on cassette,' Steve said at one point.

'Cheeky young nurd!' said George.

At eleven o'clock, Maggie made them all a cup of tea, George went home and Steve kissed her goodnight and went to bed.

It was the kind of ordinary evening that millions of women all over the country had every night. To Maggie it was a luxury.

She only wished she could have enjoyed it more, wallowed in it, but she couldn't. Something was nagging at her and she was forced, instead of simply enjoying them, consciously to use all the little details of family life that she loved so much as a deliberate distraction from the notion that was haunting her.

When the others had gone, it got worse. She did a little more work on the costume and then went to bed herself.

But not to sleep. Wheeling slowly in her mind like a giant Ferris ride was the idea she wouldn't yet admit to her consciousness.

Every time she started to slide into the warm tides of sleep, her conscious censor would relax, the images would loom and she would snap herself back to wakefulness.

She spent a wretched night, slept fitfully for the last two hours of it and got up looking and feeling dreadful, with a cracking headache.

Steve and George recognised the signs and kept a low profile over breakfast, treading quietly, making the coffee and toast for her and turning Steve's radio down to the barely audible.

Touched by their considerateness and by the contrast to the customary, clonking male noisiness she found herself smiling inside despite herself.

But the minute she got into the car, her depression descended on her again. She arrived at the station forty minutes earlier than usual and instantly called for photographs of all the victims of the rapist so far. When Jimmy arrived, comic in his astonishment at having been forestalled for once, she had them spread out on her desk.

A shutter seemed to fall down over Jimmy's face as he saw them.

Maggie didn't even bother with the preliminaries of greeting:

'Come over here, sergeant,' she said.

Jimmy seemed to cross the room as if straining against steel hawsers which were holding him back and stood next to her, silent, looking down at the pictures.

'Well?' asked Maggie.

'Pictures of the girls in the rape case,' said Jimmy.

'Full marks!' exclaimed Maggie, sarcastically. 'What else?'

'What else is there?'

'What else is there, *inspector*!' she said. If he was going to be mulish just because she'd got in before him, then sod him; he was going to have to learn that her mood wasn't of the chirpiest, either.

'Inspector,' he repeated.

'Doesn't anything strike you?' she asked.

'No . . . Inspector.'

'Think, sergeant! What did Bill Ryder say in the pub yesterday? One of the things he said is that it's possible some rapists have a type they go for. They always attack the same type.'

'Yeah, I remember.'

'Then look at the pictures again,' she said, her patience strained.

He looked, obstinately mute.

'They're all the same type!' said Maggie, bringing her fist down on the pictures exasperatedly. 'Dark hair, mostly curly, same shape of face, noticeable eyes.'

'Yeah, I suppose so,' said Jimmy.

'You suppose so? It's sticking out a mile! You'd better sharpen up, sergeant. You may look half asleep, but that's no reason for being half asleep. Now – what else do you notice?'

It was a measure of how deeply she had stung Jimmy that he replied the way he did:

'Listen, ma'am,' – he only ever used that style of address when he was really needled with her, reflected Maggie – 'Listen ma'am, it so happens I noticed it a lot sooner than you did. As soon as Ryder mentioned it. I realised all the girls were the same type. And I also tumbled the other thing, too.'

'What other thing would that be?' asked Maggie, her anger mounting.

'That it's *your* type!' Jimmy exploded. 'That's going to be your next point, isn't it? That's what I'm supposed to notice next!'

There was a deep silence as Maggie surveyed him, her face a canvas of conflicting emotions: 'You realised all this yesterday, yet you didn't see fit to pass on the fruits of your genius to a humble Inspector. Why?'

His blood was really surging now and he was very close to insubordination.

'Because I knew what your next step would be! What it's going to be now. You're going to put yourself up as a decoy!'

'What's that to you?' she asked, bluntly.

'I think it's a bleeding silly idea,' he said.

She had never before divined the depth of Jimmy's feelings of protectiveness towards her. Oh, she had known they were there; her woman's radar had told her that. But they had always been well cloaked by their formal relationship of rank, rules, tradition, form. They had been demonstrated dramatically only once or twice when Maggie had been in physical danger and Jimmy had turned into the Incredible Hulk.

One part of her was touched by this current proof of those feelings. The other part, the professional, was outraged:

'You mean you took a decision for me?' she asked, with enraged incredulity. 'You withheld a vital piece of observation from a senior officer because you didn't like what you thought she'd do with it? I think you'd better go away and have a quiet think, sergeant, see if you can get your priorities right. I think you'd better go and do it now.'

Jimmy turned and left without a word. Maggie leaned with both hands on her desk and looked first to her left, then to her right, at the same time taking a deep breath. She'd expected trouble from Chief Inspector Russell, yes. But trouble from her own sergeant! God knows she didn't want to do this anyway; she was no braver than the next woman. She didn't want to have to fight the whole of Seven Dials station as well as herself.

*

'It's not on, Forbes,' said Russell, the second she'd finished her initial pitch five minutes later, 'we're not looking for heroes.'

'And I'm not aiming to be one,' she said. 'I'll arrange back-up – everything but a helicopter gun-ship.'

'There are other women at this station who are the same type. Why does it have to be you?' He scanned her face, turning his head from side to side as if trying to pick up a signal.

'Because I'm not prepared to ask one of my girls to do it,' said Maggie.

'What if I ask one instead?'

Maggie's face closed down; 'That's your privilege, sir.'

It would also be Maggie's privilege, Russell reflected, to resent him, lose trust in him, to stop confiding in him; maybe to lose heart altogether.

A Chief's relationship with his inspectors was delicate. He had to be a kind of tyrant, but a benevolent one. He had to be careful not to crush that quality in them, whatever it was, which had made them inspectors in the first place.

He decided to play for time:

'Maybe it was a mistake to put you on it in the first place. It's an emotional issue.'

'Women are the only officers equipped to deal with rape,' said Maggie. 'They're the only ones who can possibly understand what it must be like! To be . . . used, like . . . things. Rape's up by seventy per cent in some parts of the country. Gang rape is going up. Men don't remember statistics like that, but women do.'

'I know the statistics,' commented Russell, drily.

But Maggie was now into her stride and not to be stopped, the remarkable blue eyes flashing: 'And when we get the bastards into court, what happens? They sit there smirking, no shame or remorse about what they've done. And there's some snide brief up on his hind legs, trying to win his grubby case by trying to prove the girl was a tart, or promiscuous, or was asking for it. As if what she's been through isn't enough, she's got to sit there and endure all that. She gets raped twice! Once by a man and once by the law – '

She stopped suddenly, realising that she was possibly playing right into Russell's hands on the emotional issue. She decided to go off at a tangent:

'Anyway,' she declared, 'it's got nothing to do with all that. It's a crime; it's on my patch; I'm the best person to solve it. If I don't crack it soon, the Yard are going to take it over, sure as fate. Do you want that?'

Russell had remained silent, letting the torrent flow, watching her carefully, his head weaving, probing for the waves behind the words.

'I've got a plan,' Maggie pleaded.

'What's the plan?' he asked.

'I'm convinced the whole thing revolves around "The Rendezvous" restaurant,' she said. 'It seems a good bet that, since our rapist doesn't work there, then he must be a patron. How else would he have noticed Susan Ross, watched her movements, known where she always parked her car?'

She leaned forward, trying to impress on him what she felt to be the urgency of it:

'I've got a feeling we haven't got much time,' she insisted. 'Bill Ryder says the man's getting more violent with each attack.'

'That's one more reason why I don't like the idea of you putting yourself up as a decoy duck,' said Russell. 'This is a dangerous operation. It needs meticulous planning and direction. How can you handle that part of it efficiently and lead the team while you're acting as decoy?'

'I'll work out the ground-plan, then I'll hand over co-ordination to Jake Barratt and Jimmy Fenton. They're both damn good officers; I've got complete confidence in them.'

'All right, let's leave that for now. You say the operation hinges on "The Rendezvous". Where does that fit into your plan?'

'I'm going to get a job as cloakroom girl there.'

'You're what?'

'With Susan Ross in hospital they need one; it's a perfectly logical cover and I'm in a position for the rapist to see me without suspecting anything.'

'How d'you know he'll go there again?'

'That's another of Bill Ryder's theories I buy,' said Maggie. 'This is a man who likes his food. And "The Rendezvous" is a good restaurant.'

'And it's got to be you?'

'If you've got a man who'd be a turn-on as a cloakroom girl, I'd be happy to use him, sir.'

Bill Russell sat there, steady grey eyes on her face. All kinds of considerations were passing through his mind. Her obvious emotional involvement, which was dangerous. Her intense enthusiasm, which was good. The chances of having one of his best officers hurt, or worse, which was bad. The fire he'd be in, explaining why he'd let an inspector put herself on the line if things did go wrong. Not least of all his own personal liking for Maggie and his reluctance to see her put herself in danger.

But he knew she wanted this one badly. And he reckoned she had a better chance of pulling it off than anyone else. She was a remarkable copper. All right, back that:

'What about your other work?' he asked.

'It's covered,' she said.

'You've got a week,' he said. 'Let me know when you hold your final briefing.'

'Yes, sir And thank you, sir,' said Maggie and left swiftly.

As the door closed behind her, Russell leaned back into his chair, thinking hard.

Outside, on her way back to her office, Maggie was thinking, too. She was telling herself that she must be a split personality. From the way she had sold her plan to Russell, anyone would have thought she was bursting with an unquenchable zeal to get on with it. In fact, as she well knew, she had fought hard to prevent it formulating in her mind. She had deliberately used her preoccupation with the Melody murder to distract herself from it and it was only after she had got that sewn up that she had no further excuses and the scheme had forced itself to the forefront of her mind. And once it was there, she could not ignore it.

During the interview with Russell, she had found one half of herself desperately wanting him to say yes and the other half hoping he would categorically forbid her to go ahead.

Still, there was no going back now. But what she hadn't told Russell was her intuition about the job. All decoy details were dangerous, yes. But she *knew*, in a way she couldn't explain, that this was going to be more dangerous than most.

Her mind was still in a turmoil as she entered the office she shared with Croft. He was at his desk, going through a file.

Their timing was bad, these two. He was in a mood to be conciliatory. But the tension of her confrontation with Russell, her worries about the detailed workings of her plan, plus the strange forebodings she had about its outcome all combined to make her edgy and hostile. The toxins were swirling around in her blood and she couldn't help it.

'Congratulations on the Melody murder,' he said. 'Nice job.'

'Thanks,' she said, shortly.

'How's the rape going?'

'The "alleged" victim should be out of hospital in about a week,' she answered, then mentally kicked herself: why be like that? Why rake up an old argument?'

'Look, Maggie – ' Croft started.

'I'm rather busy,' she interrupted, getting out a map of Soho. There she went again! There was no need to be like that. Maybe their vibes just didn't chime, but there was no excuse for rudeness.

He echoed her thoughts: 'There you go again,' he said. 'I wasn't being patronising – '

'Weren't you?'

'Why do you always have to make me the heavy?' he asked. 'I asked how it was going because I wanted to know.'

'You trying to tell me you care?' asked Maggie.

'Of course I care,' said Croft. 'I wouldn't be in the job if I didn't care.'

He got up and crossed to her desk, leaning forward on it on both hands:

'Listen, Maggie, I know how ugly rape can be. I did my beat training in Glasgow and the ground doesn't come any tougher than that. I handled my first case when I was twenty. Kid of fifteen said the chap next door had raped her. By the time we got there, the girl's three brothers had taken the law into their own hands – they'd gelded the poor sod and the fact was he'd never laid a finger on her. She was up the stick by her own father!'

Maggie was silent.

'I have to be damn sure there has been a rape,' Croft went on, but when I am I go in hard to nail the bastard.'

'But you always start off with the assumption that the girl's lying?' Maggie challenged him.

'Don't be so bloody daft! Of course I don't. I just try not to jump to any conclusions. It wasn't that I didn't think the Ross girl was a serious case. But you were so het up – '

'I still am,' said Maggie.

In his office, since Maggie left, Russell had been doing some thinking, too. Although it was the last thing he would ever admit to anyone, Russell was hunchy, too.

He claimed to go by the book. Facts, inference, deduction, more facts and more facts. In reality, although he might use routine to nail them down, some of his own biggest successes had come from sudden flashes of insight, or nebulous feelings of unease.

He had such a feeling now and he picked up the internal telephone.

It rang on Croft's desk: 'Right away, sir,' said Croft.

He turned to Maggie: 'We'll continue this another time,' he said.

'Yeah,' said Maggie.

Croft came into Russell's office and stood respectfully in front of his desk.

'This rape case,' asked Russell, 'has Maggie told you what she's got in mind?'

Croft grinned wryly: 'My room-mate doesn't exactly confide in me, sir,' he said.

'It's heavy,' said Russell. 'Very heavy. She's pretty well got the killing ground marked out and she's going to play the bait herself.'

Croft whistled: 'No wonder she wasn't what you might call all sweetness and light with me just now. She's got a lot on her mind. That kind of operation – '

'She's arranging her own back-up, but I've seen this kind of thing go wrong before,' Russell said. 'Too many imponderables, too many possible surprises; and by all accounts this is a dangerous bastard she's up against. So I'm going in for over-kill.' He paused and stood up, fingers on the desk: 'I want you to give her back-up, too.'

'Me!' exclaimed Croft. 'She'll climb up the curtains!'

'Then it's up to you to see that she doesn't find out, isn't it?' Russell answered.

'How am I supposed to do that?' asked Croft, aghast.

'You're a detective, full of guile and the old moody,' said Russell, with a ghost of a smile: 'You'll work something out.'

'We're chancing our arm, sir,' warned Croft.

'She's a bloody good copper,' said Russell, 'and I don't want anything to happen to her. I'll take my chances.'

Frank Angel's face was a study in outraged incredulity: 'The Fuzz?! In my restaurant? Watching everything that goes on?'

Instinctively, he covered up an accounts book that was lying open on his desk. He looked as if someone had walked out without paying. He was in his handsomely untidy office at 'The Rendezvous' with Maggie.

'Got nothing to hide, have you, Frankie?' asked Maggie, with her most innocent blue and white smile.

Frank shuffled, awkwardness fused with indignation: 'No, 'course I haven't. It's just the principle of the thing, isn't it?'

'It was an employee of yours who got raped, Frankie,' Maggie pointed out. 'Sweet little Susan. Don't you feel you've got a responsibility to help to find the sod who did it?'

'Well, yeah, I mean anything within reason,' he temporised.

She lowered her voice confidentially: 'Look, Frankie, I'm not the Inland Revenue or the VAT man: any little fiddles you get up to on their pitch are no concern of mine. We don't cross-fertilise, you know – '

'Fiddles?' bristled Frank, indignantly. 'Who said anything about fiddles?'

'All I'm saying,' she persisted, 'is there's no hot line between us. They do their job, we do ours. I'm out to catch a rapist, okay?'

'I dunno . . .' said Frank, still doubtfully.

Maggie looked dreamily out of the window: 'On the other hand,' she said, 'I do have a friendly drink now and then with the Health Inspector. Now he *can* be a bit of a nit-picker – '

Frank, who had never in his life, let pride stand in the way of self-preservation, instantly and abjectly surrendered:

'What are we talking Health Inspectors?' he asked. 'I'd be knocked out to have you as my new cloakroom girl!'

A pretty, dark girl of about twenty-eight, with a lovely, swaying walk, came in. Frank demonstrated his quick footwork:

''Morning, Di,' he said. 'This is Diane, our cashier,' he told Maggie. 'Diane,' he went on, 'this is Maggie – she's going to help us out in the cloakroom for a few days until Susan gets back.'

'Hello,' Maggie smiled.

'Hello, Maggie,' said Diane. 'Sooner you than me – all those mixed-up umbrellas.'

She had come for her float for the lunchtime trade. Frank gave it to her and she left, gracefully, with another friendly smile at Maggie.

Frank waited until she had closed the door behind her

then he turned to Maggie: 'Here, I wouldn't have to pay you, would I?'

'I'd even give you my tips,' said Maggie.

Russell insisted Maggie took the Sunday off – although she was supposed to be on turn. Nevertheless, after a lie-in and another bout of tennis with Steve in the afternoon, the evening found her in the living room with a brief-case on her lap, going through a pile of reports she had brought home with her.

George was blissfully surrounded by a paper mountain in the form of most of the Sunday papers and Steve was trying to get his hair just so in the mirror. 'Thanks for getting the detergent yesterday, Dad,' she said to George absently.

'Yes,' said George, 'we was a bit low on cereal and sugar and lemonade, too, so I topped 'em up. Got a special offer on the lemonade – supermarket own brand, 5 p off.'

'Oh, God!' exclaimed Steve.

'Listen,' said George, '5 p is 5 p.'

'That's what it tastes like, too,' said Steve, ' – without the five.'

Maggie looked up: 'Steve, don't be disgusting. Thanks Dad. I'll have to do a big shop next time I change shifts. Talking of shifts, I'm afraid I'm going to be late all this week.'

'Aw, Mum!' protested Steve, disgustedly, 'you said you'd be early all next week.'

'I would have been,' explained Maggie, 'but something's come up. You going out with whatsername tonight?' she asked, unfairly using a ploy which could infallibly be relied on to shut him up.

'Yeah . . . whatsername,' he answered, briefly. He

gave his hair a last despairing pat in the mirror, kissed her quickly and went.

'She must be a bit of all right, young whatsername,' grinned George, 'he's been at his hair for twenty minutes.'

'She is,' smiled Maggie, 'I've seen her.' She reached into her brief-case: 'By the way, if you need me next week, this is where you'll find me.' She handed George a card.

He held it at arm's length: 'What's this, then . . . "Rendezvous" restaurant? . . .'

'That's where I'll be if you want to get me urgently, any time from, say, noon until midnight.'

George revolved the name in his head: '"Rendezvous" restaurant . . . Here, ain't that where that kid was done up?'

'Susan Ross,' said Maggie. 'That's right.'

'I was just reading about it,' said George. 'Nice looking girl.'

He rustled and burrowed among his tossed and tumbled newspapers like a squirrel among leaves and came up with one carrying a picture of Susan as she looked before the attack.

'I don't know what you think you're doing messing about in that,' he grumbled, as he straightened out the paper. 'That's no job for a woman.'

'On the contrary,' she answered. 'Only a woman can crack it.'

George studied Susan's picture: 'If I was her father and I got hold of the git who did it to her . . .' He frowned: 'Funny thing – she looks a bit like you and all.'

He looked up at Maggie suddenly, before she had a chance to turn away. She had never been able to hide anything from her father, ever since she was a kid. Her face, at once guilty and aggressive, told him the whole story.

He lowered the paper slowly. He looked shaken: 'Here! You're never . . .'

'Dad, listen to me – '

George spoke as if he didn't believe his own words: 'You're never going to let yourself be a decoy!'

'I'm not *letting* myself be anything,' replied Maggie, heatedly. 'You talk as if I'm being manipulated or something. Nobody's *making* me do it. I'm in charge of the case. I've chosen to do it.'

'For God's sake, why?' asked her father.

'Well, for one thing, you said it yourself – how much like Susan Ross I look. Our doctor thinks the man we're looking for may have a type.'

George's voice shook: 'I think you're bloody stark raving mad,' he said. 'Staking yourself out for the kind of animal this sod must be.'

'Dad, it's my job.'

'So I've said it before and I'll say it again until I ain't got no oxygen left: the police is no bloody job for a woman!'

Maggie snapped back: 'And I say that any woman who's had her husband shot down by scum . . .' Her eyes strayed to the picture of her husband on the side table, in uniform, that slightly uncertain, crooked smile and her eyes started to prickle; the familiar ache started at the back of her throat; would she ever stop feeling like this? '. . . I'm entitled to hit back, to carry on the war against the bastards in his name . . . to feel he's . . . a bit less dead because of it.'

She started to get the sniffles: 'Oh, damn!' She got out a tissue.

George never could bear to see her cry: 'Don't do that, there's a good gel,' he pleaded, shattered; 'makes me corns ache.'

Maggie smiled despite herself: 'Any more out of you and I'll stamp on them.'

George heaved himself out of his chair and came towards her. He had the same look of care and protectiveness on his face that she remembered seeing there all her life:

'Listen, Maggie, love,' he started.

Maggie forced a grin. 'Dad!' she cried, warningly, pretending she was about to stamp on his foot.

'No,' said her father, 'nothing more. 'Nuff said. No, it's just that I mean . . . well . . . you will be careful, won't you?'

Maggie reached out and hugged this dear man who, she knew, worried every time she went out to work until she came back:

'Listen,' she said, 'I *have* got a team of big, strong men to look after me, you know.'

Next morning Maggie woke up with the tension wound up inside her like the jam in a Swiss roll. When she got in she checked her desk, then went straight around the corner to the gym that the more energetic members of the station used. Hard, punishing exercise was the best tranquilliser she knew.

She had taken Jimmy with her; he was a keep-fit fanatic beneath the indolent manner. He looked up at her now from the corner where he'd been pounding out squat-thrusts.

She was hanging from the wall-bars in a leotard the colour of her eyes, slowly bringing her knees up to her chest.

In here, as in 'The Tank', rank was left outside: 'Here,' said Jimmy, his eyes shining, 'do that one again.'

'You just keep your eyes down and get on with your own sweating,' she said.

Jimmy grinned: 'Pity you're not going to be the sort of hat-check girl you see in the old movies; all fishnet tights and black seams.'

Maggie lowered herself gracefully from the bars: 'I'll

wear that,' she said, 'if you put on a bellboy's uniform and a little round pill-box hat. Come on, time to get back to the factory.'

Her plan was to put in lunch-times at 'The Rendezvous' just in case, which she very much doubted, The Frog was a luncher there rather than a diner, handle her other outstanding cases in the afternoon, then go back for the evening session.

She had bought herself a low-cut blouse and a much tighter skirt than anything in her wardrobe, but she did not intend to wear them until the evening. Nor was she going to deploy the back-up team until nightfall; nothing was going to happen in the middle of the day.

Nothing did. Frank Angel showed her the child's-play cloakroom system, the patrons streamed in gratefully from the steam-heat pavements – June still seemed determined to grill London to a crisp. Maggie, just in case, studied every man who came in. But what was she looking for? What does a rapist look like? It's not stamped on his forehead.

It was an eerie experience, looking into the succession of faces, knowing that one of them could possibly be The Frog, the obscene freak who had done the vile things that were written down, in details, in bad police typing, in the reports at Seven Dials.

Lunchtime was uneventful, as she had expected it to be. She had a few mild passes made at her, but nothing more than she was accustomed to normally. Dinner, evening, twilight shading into thick darkness, that was the atmosphere the thing she hunted preferred, both practically and – she knew by instinct – emotionally. He was a hunter of the night. But now he had become the hunted. How would he feel if he knew? she wondered.

She went back to the station and interviewed a man who had been taken from his bed at 6 a.m. that morning in connection with the robbery of the Jermyn Street jewellers. The tip had come from Ron, in Berwick Market, as he had promised.

By this time chummy had his solicitor with him, a well-known bent-mouth who'd have needed a ladder to reach up and scratch the underbelly of a snake. He was in some little difficulty this time, however, because two pieces of the stolen jewellery – heavy gold bracelets – had been found cleverly hidden in his client's garage, held delicately between the jaws of a vice, with a cloth draped over it. Bent-mouth was finding it hard to make his usual routine accusation of 'plant' sound credible.

By the time Maggie had handed over to Jimmy while she went for a cup of tea and a biscuit in the canteen, he was starting to hint at a spot of plea-bargaining. Her answer had been short, flat and negative. Before she'd finished with him and his client they'd be offering names – it had been a four-handed job. That was the time to offer a little easement.

As the time approached for her to go back to 'The Rendezvous' for the dinner session she could feel the springs tightening in her stomach again. She took the clothes she had bought and changed into them in the Ladies.

She also put more lipstick and eye shadow on than usual and more colour on her cheeks.

As she came out and passed through the CID room, something like an electric current seemed to pass around it, causing detectives to sit bolt upright in their chairs. A certain flashing of the blue eyes, however, told them that it would be a rash man who let the wolf-whistle, which was trembling behind every pair of lips, escape.

In her office, Jake and Jimmy were poring over a map on her desk:

'We'll have men posted here and there,' Jake was

saying 'That way they'll all have a good view of the restaurant.'

'I'll take the booth,' said Jimmy.

'And Derek and Jack will keep obbo on the waste-ground . . .'

Jake tailed off as he saw Jimmy staring fixedly past his right shoulder.

He turned to see Maggie in her tight skirt, high heels, low-cut blouse and heightened make-up. 'Blimey!' he said. 'Have you got a licence to drive that lot?'

'And if so,' added Jimmy, 'how many endorsements has it got?'

Dressed the way she was and looking the way she did, she knew there was no way she could pull rank on them. And although she was slightly angry and self-conscious, she warmed to the frank admiration on their faces: 'All right,' she said, 'turn it down. Let's have the comedy auditions later, shall we?'

Jimmy and Jake dutifully straightened their faces: 'Now then, let's get on with it – '

Croft came in, his hot brown eyes appraising her expertly and appreciatively: 'Well, if that doesn't pull him, nothing will,' he said. 'Mind you . . .'

'Well?' asked Maggie, waiting for the sting in the tail.

'If you do get him, a smart Defence Counsel could plead incitement,' he added.

'Thanks a bunch. Next time send me a memo,' said Maggie.

Croft grinned and went over to his desk. He sat down and began pecking out a report on his typewriter with two fingers. He rapidly became apparently totally absorbed.

'All right,' Maggie told the other two, 'you can start getting your people into position. Jimmy, you go first, then you and the others, Jake, at five minute intervals. I'll be getting to the restaurant at seven sharp.'

On the outside, she was the cool, efficient policewoman they were used to seeing. Inside, her stomach was churning like a concrete mixer:

'All right, let's get rolling,' she said.

'Good hunting,' said Croft, a little absently, as they left the office.

He waited a few minutes for them to get clear of the building, then he got up, jingling his car keys.

Maggie drove to the car park near the restaurant, the same one in which Susan had been raped. She drove in. Jimmy greeted her respectfully from the attendant's booth. 'Evenin', miss!'

'Hello,' smiled Maggie.

'Be long, will you, miss?'

'Probably 'til about midnight.'

'That'll be 60 p.'

She paid him and got her ticket: 'Right at the back there, if you don't mind, miss.'

'Thanks,' said Maggie and pulled into a space against the far wall, where Susan Ross used to park.

As she walked out, Jimmy shouted to her: 'I'll leave the gates open for you if you're late, miss.'

'Thanks,' said Maggie. She crossed Dean Street and went on into 'The Rendezvous'.

On a corner of Romilly Street opposite the car park a layabout hung around, scuffling his feet, hands in the pockets of his bomber jacket. Jimmy stuck his head out of his booth and twisted around. He and the layabout exchanged nods that would not have been perceptible to an outsider.

Jimmy shifted his glance. On the opposite corner a scruff in filthy jeans, sweat shirt and sneakers, exchanged the same sort of nod with him.

The original man-in-a-dirty-raincoat turned away

from the window of a pornographic bookshop. He, too, exchanged the signal with Jimmy.

Halfway up Romilly Street, Jake sat in an unmarked car.

And on a rooftop overlooking the whole scene, unknown to anyone, Inspector Bob Croft crouched, with a light-enhancing night 'scope.

In 'The Rendezvous' the diners came in three waves: the pre-theatre crowd, who couldn't sit through a show with their stomachs rumbling, the post-theatre crowd, who had done just that and the parties who were making the meal itself their night out.

There were also a few regulars, people who lived or had businesses locally and who found it convenient to dine there, mostly choosing the economical dish of the day and a half-carafe of house wine.

They tended to be on their own.

There was one man who attracted Maggie's attention. There was something mutedly sinister about him. He was well-dressed and not an obvious thug, but you wouldn't, Maggie considered, leave your daughter alone with him. Nor your son.

As he had handed in a shower-proof mac when he came in, he had wordlessly inspected Maggie with his coal-black eyes in a way which she had found frankly disconcerting.

At the moment, he was sitting at a corner table on his own and doing himself very well. No dish of the day for him: he was going through the card, with a bottle of good wine on the table. He was engrossed in his food.

Maggie was peering in at him now with Frank by her side.

'Know anything about him?' Maggie was asking.

'Only that his name's Stringer,' Frank answered. 'Why?'

Maggie shrugged: 'Nothing I can pin down. It's just that I don't like the look of him. Can you remember, was he here the night Susan Ross was attacked?'

Frank thought hard: 'Yeah . . . yeah, I reckon he was. Don't mean much, though. He's one of my medium reg'lars; he's in a lot.'

The after-theatre assault was just starting and it coincided with the exodus of many of those who had come in earlier. For a while, Maggie was fully occupied taking in, ticketing and returning coats, hats, umbrellas, brief-cases, even – in one case – a copy of 'The Times' from a man who hadn't yet finished the crossword.

Now it had slackened off and she was attending to the only other man who, besides Stringer, was there by himself that night.

Frank had told her his name was Owen. He had strikingly handsome eyes and a beautifully modulated, cultured voice.

As she handed him his expensive, velvet-collared coat, he was making a smooth and practised play for her:

'Thank you. You're new, aren't you?' he asked.

Maggie smiled at him. She felt like smiling at him, to be honest: 'Just temporary,' she answered.

'And what time do you finish, Miss Temporary?' asked Owen, the handsome eyes doing it all for him.

'When the last customer's got his coat,' said Maggie. 'Then I pick up my husband from his karate school.'

Owen conceded with a smile as charming as her own: 'Goodnight, Miss Temporary,' he said.

'Goodnight, sir,' said Maggie. She looked after him a little wistfully, then turned back to the racks of coats and belongings.

In the next instant, she heard a noise behind her. She turned quickly to find Stringer there, the black eyes boring into hers.

He handed her his ticket without speaking and without taking his eyes off hers.

She handed him his coat. He took it, turned and went. He still hadn't uttered a word.

Gradually, the tempo slackened, the restaurant emptied, the waiters began to look pointedly at the hangers-on. Finally, they were all gone.

Diane, the cashier with the dark hair and the pretty walk, came through, got her coat herself from a hanger near Maggie:

'Did you manage, Maggie?' she asked.

'Just about,' grinned Maggie. 'You all cashed up?'

'And balanced, thank God,' said Diane. 'See you tomorrow, Maggie.'

''Night, Diane. Take care.'

Diane went. Maggie shrugged into her own coat, said goodnight to Frank and stepped out into the night. The lounging detectives outside, beginning to get bored now that they no longer had faces to study and remember as patrons came and went, snapped into alertness.

In his attendant's booth, Jimmy was crouched out of sight.

Up the street, Jake switched on the engine of his car.

And on the roof Croft, playing his lone game, put his night 'scope to his eye.

Maggie walked to her car against the back wall. It was the last one left. The scrunch, scrunch, scrunch of her own footsteps sounded deafening in her ears. She felt as if she were walking to her doom.

She reached her car, unlocked it and drove out of the car park. Nothing whatsoever happened.

Nothing happened, in fact, the following night either, nor the night after that, nor the night after that. Stringer came in every night with his baleful stare. The good-looking Owen came in twice more. The look-outs were mounted, the adrenalin was switched on, but it looked as if they were on the biggest anti-climax of all time.

Then, on the Friday night, they were left covered in egg from head to feet. Two streets away from 'The Rendezvous', Diane was attacked on her way home. She was walking along the deserted pavement when an arm shot out of a dark alley, crooked around her throat and dragged her back into the deep darkness of the alley, heels thrashing.

Luckily, she got out one tremendous scream which, even more fortunately, was heard by the uniformed Stewart and Miller, just turning the corner on their regular patrol, in their Panda car.

They screamed up, siren blasting, to find Diane sobbing on the ground with a sprained arm and a swollen face, but not a sign of the hooded figure she described as having attacked her.

Half an hour later Maggie had Jimmy, Jake and the three 'layabouts' in front of her desk. Her eyes were blazing:

'Five of you right on the spot and he walks through you! I know he came from the blind side and I know we were expecting someone else, but for God's sake you'd think that *one* of you might have stumbled over him on your way home!'

'Ma'am – ' said Jimmy.

Maggie cut him off: 'Give me generals who are lucky – that's what Napoleon used to say and this morning I know exactly what he meant.'

'Chief – ' said Jake.

Maggie steam-rollered on: 'Yes, I know I'm being unfair. Well, I feel like being un-bloody-fair! Russell's on duty and I have to go in and face him. What am I supposed to tell him? How do I defend our operation?'

Five minutes later, she was in front of Russell and doing her best:

'At least she wasn't sexually assaulted, sir,' she said.

'No thanks to you and your lot,' replied Russell. 'What if the Panda hadn't happened to be there? And you're still no further on.'

'I disagree, sir,' said Maggie. 'At least we know for sure that our man is somehow connected with that restaurant. Two girls from the same place can't be coincidence. And I have a suspect.'

'A suspect!' said Russell. 'Why didn't you say so. Let's have him in and shake him 'til he rattles.'

'He's not a suspect in that sense,' said Maggie. 'I've got nothing to go on. It's just a customer who's . . . creepy.'

Russell spoke with a flatness you could have measured with a spirit level: 'Creepy.'

'If you were a woman you'd know what I mean,' said Maggie.

Russell paused, his eyes like flints: 'I do know this,' he said. 'You can't afford to spend any more time personally trailing your coat in that restaurant, putting yourself up as bait to a rapist who may or may not be there. Set up a routine surveillance and get on with the rest of your work. After this latest attack the Yard will probably take over anyway.'

Maggie put everything she'd got into her plea. She knew she was close. She couldn't let it go now. 'Look, sir; tomorrow's Saturday. I'm off duty. I'd like to give it one more go tomorrow night. My men are off, too, but they've volunteered to go along with it. Our man didn't get what he wanted tonight; the odds are he'll have another go. This time there'll be no slip-ups, I swear.'

She knew Russell would find it difficult to deny her the chance to work in her spare time. She saw the eyes flicker and followed up with a deliberate piece of impudent confidence: 'Oh, and I'd also like to borrow the police surgeon.'

'Anything else?' asked Russell. 'I mean, you wouldn't like to ask the Yard for their computer as well?'

As soon as Maggie heard the trace of flippancy in his voice, although his face remained rigorously straight, she knew she'd won. To those who knew Russell – and it took some considerable time to achieve that knowledge – that subtle variation of tone meant yes.

'No, thank you, sir,' said Maggie, slightly cocky with relief, 'computers aren't very strong on psychology.'

'I didn't hear that word, Inspector,' said Russell. 'You'd better get out before I do.'

She grabbed Bill Ryder just as he was on his way home, having made his medical report on Diane and put the proposition to him:

'At last!' shouted Ryder, theatrically. Our first dinner together. I thought you'd never ask! And what's even better – you're paying!'

Maggie smiled. 'We won't be having it together,' she said, patiently, knowing that he knew perfectly well they wouldn't be. 'I'll be running the cloakroom as usual. You'll be watching a man.'

'Oh goody,' said Ryder, sourly, 'that's my favourite pastime!'

'Bill, he's odd,' said Maggie. 'You'll be watching him as a doctor. If you can give me any kind of professional opinion that he could be our man I'll find some excuse to haul him in and roast him.'

'Don't build your hopes too high, Maggie,' warned Ryder. 'There's no particular rapist style of eating.'

Maggie changed the subject: 'How's Diane?'

'She'll be fine,' said Bill. 'There was no need to leave her at the hospital, so I've brought her back so she can give you her statement.

'She's in your office, dictating it to a WPC. I called

her husband to take her home. He's up in the canteen having a cup of tea,' Bill concluded.

'He could have stayed with her,' said Maggie, 'I wouldn't have minded.'

'I thought it was better my way,' replied Bill. 'You'll see what I mean.'

As Maggie went into her office, Diane, a purplish bruise around her throat, was awkwardly signing her statement with her strapped-up arm.

She looked up, saw Maggie and handed her the statement.

'Thanks, love,' said Maggie, her face serious.

'I should have guessed you were police,' said Diane. 'Frank didn't tell me.'

'I asked him not to,' said Maggie; 'we wanted every one to act normally.'

Diane smiled ruefully: 'And here was I, carefully keeping off the subject of Susan so as not to upset you.'

'I appreciated it all the same,' said Maggie. 'And I'm so sorry about what happened to you.'

'It wasn't your fault. I think what you're doing is fantastic. I hope you get him.'

'Susan says she hopes I don't,' said Maggie.

'What?! After what she went through?'

'That's her point,' explained Maggie. 'She doesn't want to have to go through it all again, giving evidence at his trial. She lives in dread of having to tell all those strange faces the . . . terrible things she had to tell me.'

'That's it,' said Diane, thoughtfully, 'that's the awful thing: it doesn't just stop with the attack.' She grimaced ironically: 'I find I've got a problem, too. It's a bit different to Diane's.'

'What is it?'

'Well, I won't be working at the restaurant any more for a start. My husband's made that quite clear. When he came to fetch me tonight he could see the state I was in, but all he wanted to know was if the attacker had managed to . . . well . . . you know. Even when I told him he hadn't, Jack still didn't really believe me until he'd had a word with your doctor. It was as if he'd suddenly stopped trusting me. As if I was somehow . . . tainted.'

'He'll come around,' Maggie told her, reassuringly: 'it's just that it's been a hell of a shock for him, too. Maybe he feels guilty for not taking better care of you.'

'Could be,' said Diane. 'I suppose I'll just have to be patient with him.' Again her ironic smile: '*I'll* have to be patient with *him*!'

She got up to go: 'Well, good luck!'

The WPC opened the door for her. In the doorway she paused and turned:

'I've just remembered something: the man . . . he wore scent.'

'What? Aftershave – that sort of thing?'

'Yes, I suppose it was. Smelled of lemons,' said Diane. 'Hope it helps.'

'Everything helps,' said Maggie.

Diane went and Maggie shrugged wearily into her coat. It was nearly a quarter to two and she felt bushed. Jake, who lived in the next road to hers, came in, took one look at her: 'I'm driving you home,' he said. 'You can leave your motor here and I'll bring you in again tomorrow.'

She was too tired to argue: 'Thanks, Jake,' she answered gratefully, the shutters sliding down over her eyes in a slow blink.

It was two thirty as they drove up to Maggie's house.

All the lights were on:

'Funny,' said Maggie. 'Steve should have been in bed hours ago!'

'I'll come in with you,' said Jake.

Maggie opened the door and they went in. In the middle of the living room, all the lights blazing, stood Steve.

His face looked so like Bob's in a foul mood that her heart turned over.

She believed in attacking first: 'What are you doing still up?' she demanded.

'I was worried,' Steve hit back, flatly.

This was going to be no walk-over, thought Maggie; go in hard, girl:

'Don't be ridiculous,' she snapped, 'I've been this late before!'

Steve's eyes swept up and down Maggie from head to toe: 'Not dressed like that, you haven't,' he said.

With a sudden shock of dismay Maggie realised that, in her tiredness, she had forgotten to change back out of the slightly tarty outfit she had worn at the restaurant and to restore her make-up to its usual muted understatement.

Jake stepped in to her rescue: 'Your Mum and me decided to forget we were coppers for a few hours and have a night out on the town,' he said. 'I'm afraid we overdid it a bit.' He tried a joke: 'It's a wonder we weren't nicked on the way home.'

As the words were leaving his mouth, he knew it was a mistake. Steve froze him with a face like the Medusa on a bad day:

'Where did you go?' he asked, eyeing Maggie once again, 'Raymond's Revue Bar? And were you on stage or off?'

Maggie turned to Jake. It was unfair to involve him in all of this; he was a poor liar and he looked acutely embarrassed:

'Jake,' she said, 'I've taken advantage of you enough. Thanks for driving me home. I'll be ready for you bright and early in the morning.'

'Fine, Maggie,' he said. 'See you then. G'night. G'night, Steve.'

'Goodnight, Mr Barratt,' Steve answered, deliberately denying him the familiar 'Jake'.

Jake left with grateful speed.

Maggie decided her only chance was to go on the attack again: 'How dare you criticise the way I dress and the way I look,' she said, 'especially in front of someone else. How dare you question what time I get home? Just who the hell do you think you are?'

'Aw, Mum,' answered Steve, in a tone that almost suggested he was disappointed in her, 'give it a rest, why don't you? D'you really think I'm that thick? D'you think I don't know what you've been up to all week? Grandpa prowling around every night like a cat on a hot stove, not even reading his paper?'

He went over and snatched from a pile the paper in which Susan Ross's picture appeared:

'D'you think I can't spot a likeness when I see one? D'you think I don't know police tactics by now? D'you really think I haven't cottoned on to the way your mind works? I practically knew before you did what you were going to do. It would have helped . . . just a bit . . . if you'd told me.'

Maggie knew she'd been blown, no point in dissembling. She was bright; she'd borne a bright son.

She spoke quietly: 'I was going to tell you, after . . .'

'There might not have been an after,' said Steve, bitterly. 'There was no "after" for Dad.'

'Steve,' said Maggie, trying to lower the temperature, 'it's not as bad as that – '

'It is, it bloody is,' cried Steve. 'I know the man you're up against; it's The Frog . . . the bloody Frog . . . I read the papers, I'm not a dummy. But why you? You're an Inspector; why you?'

Maggie tried to explain: 'It has to be me, Steve. I'm

the right type . . . and how can I ask one of my girls to do something I'm afraid – '

'It's horrible,' Steve exploded, 'bloody horrible!'

Maggie, shaken by his reaction, spoke to him with a force and a sincerity to which she had never exposed him before. But now suddenly she realised that he was growing up, fast and it was time he faced some of the realities that entailed:

'Sit down, Steve,' she said. She sat next to him.

'Yes, it *is* horrible,' she admitted 'and that's why I have to do it. Since I joined the Force I've worked on every kind of case – murderers, baby-bashers, GBH, the lot. I've seen things no one should have to see. But, for me, rape is the worst of the lot.' Steve looked at her.

'Murder . . . yes . . . is terrible. But . . . somehow . . . well, at least the victim is dead: you can be more detached. But when a woman has been raped she's . . . well, she's been murdered, in a way. Part of her has been killed, but she's still alive. Sometimes she never gets over it; it ruins the rest of her life.'

Steve was still silent. She stopped, not quite knowing how to go on, whether she'd got through:

'Steve,' she said, hesitantly, 'when you said that about it being horrible – you sounded . . . you're not ashamed of me, are you?'

'Of course not!' cried Steve. 'How can you say that? It's just that – '

'Steve, when your father died, I wanted to leave the Force then. I reasoned that if anything happened to me . . . You remember what you said then?'

'Yes.'

'You told me not to use you as an excuse to quit the job. So I took you at your word.'

Steve paused, seeing the justice of her argument: 'I suppose I never thought you'd have to do anything like this,' he answered finally.

'It's all part of the same job, love,' said Maggie.

'The worst part,' he said.

'Look,' she said, 'I've only been given one more go at it. If I don't crack it tomorrow, I've got to drop it anyway. You can bear with me for twenty-four hours now, can't you?'

She forced a smile, forcing one on to his face too.

'I suppose I just might manage it,' he said.

'Good lad,' she said. 'Incidentally, I've practically got the Brigade of Guards looking after me on this caper, you know; I'm no fool.'

She couldn't know but, in the event, even the Brigade of Guards wouldn't have been of much help.

He shaved himself lovingly with an old-fashioned cut-throat razor, the beautifully self-manicured hands sweeping the cheeks and chin smooth with carefully rhythmical strokes.

On a glass shelf nearby in the scrubbed and gleaming bathroom stood a cassette-recorder.

It was playing a 'Teach Yourself French' tape.

'I would like a croissant and some butter, please,' intoned the tape. '*Je voudrais un croissant et du beurre, s'il vous plait.*'

'*Je voudrais un croissant et du beurre, s'il vous plait,*' he repeated, happily, his accent pretty close.

'I'll be home early . . . *Je vais rentrer a la bonne heure,*' said the cassette.

'*Je vais rentrer a la bonne heure,*' he repeated, scraping deftly into the little delve in the middle of his chin.

'My sweetheart . . . *ma cherie,*' said the cassette.

'*Ma cherie,*' he imitated, pursing his lips at himself in the mirror.

He levelled off his sideboards with the precision of a guillotine:

'My little cabbage,' recited the cassette, '*Mon p'tit choux.*'

'*Mon p'tit choux*,' he repeated with a final flourish of the razor and a dazzling smile at himself in the mirror.

He wiped the residual lather from his face with a towel, drenched his hands with his favourite after-shave and patted it on to his shorn and pristine cheeks.

It smelled of lemon.

In the Ladies at Seven Dials Maggie was finishing the heavy laying-on of the lipstick and touching up her hair. She was wearing the same body-hugging, skin-revealing ensemble that had so upset Steve the night before.

She came out and called her team together in her office.

'Right,' she said, to Jimmy, Jake and the three layabouts, 'this is our last chance. Either we have him over tonight or the Yard take over – and none of us want that – right?'

'Right!' was the universal response.

'Fine,' said Maggie, 'so it's the same game-plan that we've used all week – with one exception: when Stringer leaves, I want him tailed. Grange, that's down to you, right?' The detective whom she'd singled out nodded:

'Yes, ma'am.'

'I want to know where he goes almost before he gets there – right?'

'Right, ma'am,' said Grange.

'And I want you to stay with him to see if he comes out again. If he does, you're to let Sergeant Barratt know immediately on your walkie-talkie and stay with him. Is that clear?'

'Quite clear, ma'am,' said Grange.

The beautiful hand reached out and selected a favourite suit from the wardrobe and a fine lawn shirt. It also selected one or two other items that could be left in the car until the time was right.

He dressed himself with great care. After all, this was his pleasure that he was about and a man's pleasures should be taken seriously. And this was going to be the very peak and perfection of his vicious, hedonistic career so far. This was what it had all been about.

Croft was on duty this Saturday and able to show himself at Seven Dials openly without Maggie wondering why he was there.

Scrubbed and immaculate as usual, he came into the office without making a fuss, took no notice of Maggie and her team, but immediately dialled a number on his telephone and started speaking.

The number was non-existent; there was no one on the other end of the line. In the long pauses he engineered he listened to every word of Maggie's briefing.

Maggie finished and her team trooped out to take up their positions. Croft didn't hurry. He had plenty of time:

'This it, then, is it?' he asked her.

'Well, if we're ever going to bag him it's going to be tonight,' she said. 'For one thing it's my last chance and for another it's psychologically right. He was frustrated last night; it's likely he'll have another go tonight. Most of all I feel it, I know he's on his way, I can sense him moving in.'

Croft said nothing. He knew that normally Maggie wouldn't have dreamed of confiding in him like this about one of her cases, but he realised that her nerves were stretched; she needed to unload on someone.

'D'you know what I think?' she said. 'I think he's an arrogant sod. I think he's somehow sussed that I'm the law; that's why he tried Diane last night, not me. Why else would he do that? Going by his other victims I'm much more his type than Diane was, so why pick her?'

'If that's true,' said Croft, 'why should he go for you tonight? If he suspects you're the law he must know what a risk he's running.'

'I told you,' said Maggie, 'he's frustrated and he's arrogant. He'd probably get an extra kick out of the chanciness of it.'

Again Croft was silent. She slung a light raincoat over her blouse and skirt and went.

Croft went in to see Russell: 'I'm taking another man,' he said. 'He can stay on the roof; I want to be on the ground.'

The evening trade at 'The Rendezvous' had built up to its peak. Stringer was in, his long, delicate fingers cracking lobster claws at his usual table. The sleekly handsome Owen was in, his striking eyes flicking now and then towards the opening through which Maggie could be seen.

Bill Ryder was in a commanding position against the wall. An old and valued customer of 'The Rendezvous', he was giving the à la carte a caning on police funds the like of which Frank Angel had never seen before – and he'd seen Bill Ryder treat himself to some Lucullan feasts in his time.

Maggie peeked at him now and then, her irritation mounting as she saw him apparently far more interested in his stomach than he was in assessing Stringer.

At one juncture, she caught his eye and inclined her head impatiently to where Stringer was sitting, composed, still and sinister as ever.

Bill nodded amiably and addressed himself to soaking

up the garlic butter from his snails with his fluffy-centred, crisply crusted French bread.

She looked at him again ten minutes later. He was still eating busily the way a Frenchman eats, all action, breaking bread, sipping wine, reaching for butter, mixing salad dressing.

She was there watching him so long that Frank found himself having to cope with a sudden rush of coats. He climbed into his pseudo-Italian voice: 'Hey, Maggie! You want-a to come and-a help me with-a da coats, eh?'

'Sorry, Mr Angelo,' answered Maggie. She came and sorted things out, relieved to see that Ryder had at least just shot a glance across at Stringer.

The rush subsided, Frank mopped his brow and quietly confided his worries to Maggie: 'Blimey, if my customers was to find out what's going on in here tonight, there'd be a stampede for the bleeding doors!'

'Frankie, there's nothing going on that need worry you,' said Maggie. 'You want this pig caught, don't you?'

'Yeah, but – '

'Well then,' she concluded with irrefutable, if understated, logic.

'I can't stand it,' he said, 'I'm taking an early night. Giuseppe can look after things.' He handed over to Giuseppe, a solidly built young man who really was Italian, and went, his finely tailored back as he passed out through the door expressing relief.

Maggie turned back to find that Stringer had once again taken her by surprise. He was standing there, motionless, holding out his cloakroom ticket, the jet eyes never wavering.

He took his coat, dropped his tip into the saucer and left without a word.

Maggie shivered.

Outside, Grange, the detective who had been detailed for the job, fell into a loitering tail in his layabout clothes behind him.

Maggie waited with growing restlessness for Bill Ryder to finish his meal. He spooned up the last of his glazed layered peaches with Chantilly cream, lingered over a coffee and a Delamain brandy, finally wiped his mouth lovingly with his napkin, paid his bill and came out.

He patted his stomach with a deep sigh of satisfaction. He exuded a unique fragrance, compounded of garlic and after-shave:

'That's one of the best blow-outs I've had in years,' he said. 'I went through the card.'

'So I noticed,' commented Maggie, dryly.

'And all at the Department's expense,' he added, luxuriously.

Maggie fretted with impatience: 'What did you make of *Stringer*?' she demanded.

'Could well be,' said Ryder. 'Something very off there. I'll let you have a report. I should tell your boys to keep an eye on him.'

In Old Compton Street Stringer was approaching a pornographic cinema club. It specialised in particularly raw sado-masochistic material. He entered with a proprietorial air, nodding briefly to the doorman-cum-minder:

'How's it been?' he asked.

'Bit quiet tonight, boss,' answered the doorman.

The exchange was heard by the layabout, who was slowly drifting by. He walked a few yards further along, stepped into a doorway and spoke to Jake on his walkie-talkie:

'He's a porn baron,' he said. 'Looks like he's in for the night.'

'Stay outside, all the same,' said Jake.

In 'The Rendezvous', Ryder was taking his leave: 'You staying long?' he asked Maggie.

'No, there's only a few lingerers left,' said Maggie. 'Shouldn't think they'll hang on.'

'I'll have that report for you by Monday,' said Ryder.

'Thanks, Bill,' said Maggie.

He went out, deliberately avoided looking towards the booth in the car park where he knew Jimmy to be concealed, ignored equally the other scruffy members of the Force he encountered on his way down Dean Street and disappeared into Shaftesbury Avenue, presumably to look for a taxi.

Twenty minutes later the last customer had gone. It was the handsome Owen, in his Savile Row suit and hand-made shirt:

'Still going home with your Black Belt husband, Miss Temporary?' he asked.

'I'm afraid so,' she said, with genuine regret.

He smiled, tipped and left.

Maggie slipped on her light coat and once more started the walk from Romilly Street across Dean Street to the car park.

She entered the car park, her heart beginning to thump. Scrunch, scrunch, scrunch across the rough surface.

By the apparently empty booth she stopped, ostensibly to shake a bit of gravel out of her high-heeled sandal. Jimmy, out of sight in the booth, whispered: 'Stringer owns a porn film club just down the road. He's home for the night.'

Maggie said nothing, walked on towards her car where it stood in the inky blackness against the far wall, where the gap-toothed fracture was.

She opened her car and climbed in, alert for the slightest movement behind her. Nothing happened. She settled into the seat, slid the key into the ignition. She had a lunatic sensation of disappointment, mixed with a tide of relief.

She slammed the door and fastened her seat belt.

A voice spoke from behind her; a beautiful, cultivated voice, disguised by an overlay of hoarseness: 'There's a gun pointing at your spine,' it said, in an almost friendly tone. 'One move I don't like and I'll blow it in half. Just drive out of here – and make it natural.'

She twisted round, caught a half glimpse of a hooded figure, crouched on the floor behind her:

'No, don't turn round,' said the voice, 'just drive.'

Maggie reversed, manoeuvred, then drove slowly out of the car park:

'Wave to your friend in the booth,' said the voice, as they passed it. Obediently, she waved to Jimmy who, relaxed now, was in the process of straightening up. He waved back.

She drove down Dean Street, Jimmy following the car casually with his eyes.

Suddenly, he frowned.

Maggie was turning right into Shaftesbury Avenue, but instead of her right indicator, her hazard lights were flashing. Maggie didn't make mistakes like that.

Jimmy opened up the channel to Jake on his walkie-talkie:

'Jake, there's something wrong. Maggie's got her hazard lights going.'

Jake's car screamed down Dean Street and picked up Jimmy at the car park entrance.

Croft, who'd kept his own receiver open, was already driving fast down Romilly Street. He stopped to pick up his sergeant, who had scrambled down from the roof with his 'scope. It might have been a very different story if he hadn't.

Maggie was driving down Shaftesbury Avenue towards Piccadilly Circus:

'Drive to Hyde Park,' said the voice behind her.

'It'll be closed,' she said.

'Not yet, it won't,' said the voice.

All around her there were cars, people thronging the pavements crossing the roads:

'What if I just stop and get out now?' she challenged.

'You'd never make it,' answered the voice, chillingly.

She went into the one-way system around the Circus then down Haymarket into Pall Mall.

She had glimpsed in her mirror the familiar sight of Jake's car about eight or nine vehicles behind, then she'd lost him. But at least it was some comfort to know he was there.

She made to take the left turn past St James's Palace into the Mall, knowing that the width of the wide, pink boulevard up to the Palace would give Jake a chance to take the intervening vehicles and pull in front. 'No,' said the voice, 'up St James's and out into Piccadilly.'

Behind, Jake and Jimmy were sweating with frustration. They daren't use their siren to bull their way through for fear of endangering Maggie and they couldn't thread their way through the tangle of late night traffic. It was only luck that allowed them to see, way ahead, Maggie's car turn right into St James's.

Croft was even further behind. All he could do was to try and keep Jake in sight.

'Faster,' said the voice as Maggie turned into Piccadilly towards Hyde Park Corner.

They sped towards the vast complex of the Hyde Park roundabout, Maggie trying to make difficulties for herself and get jammed. But, perversely, the traffic parted like magic and she had no alternative but to speed through. She could feel the gun, which her kidnapper had now jammed into the side of her ribs.

'Take Rotten Row,' he said.

She swerved round the intersection and turned left into the park, Rotten Row on her right, still curiously denuded-looking after the massacre of the trees that used to border it by Dutch Elm disease a couple of years before.

She could no longer see Jake in her mirror. She prayed for a red light at the left turn under the arch at Bowater House, but it remained obstinately green.

At Hyde Park corner, Jake was blasting a German touring coach, which had got itself hopelessly lost and was undecided whether to turn right, left or upwards. He finally pulled out into a hurtling stream of traffic on his left and passed it, leaving a near-disaster of swerving, braking and bumping cars behind him.

Maggie was now abreast of Knightsbridge Barracks on her left.

Without warning, the voice said, 'Sharp right!'

'What are you talking about?' she snapped, at breaking point, 'we'll go off the road.'

'Quite,' said the voice, emphasising the point with a jab in the ribs with the gun.

She swerved across the road, bumped over the kerb, across the pavement, across the soft sandiness of Rotten Row itself and into the grass and trees of the unlighted park.

'Switch your lights off,' said the voice, 'and keep going.'

She did as she was told and rolled deeper into the blackness of the park.

Jake finally screeched round into the park. The road ahead was clear. Of Maggie's car there was no sign. He raced right up the road, touching eighty to the turn into Knightsbridge and Kensington Gore. Nothing. He did a screaming U-turn and came roaring back. He met Croft coming in the other direction. Both cars screamed to a stop and the four men jumped out, bewildered.

Deep into the park the voice said 'Stop'. Maggie stopped. 'Get out. Slowly.'

She got out. The hooded figure got out behind her. She could see him now, bizarre, the blank head, the blank sweater, the starshine gleaming on the barrel of the automatic levelled at her.

'Into the trees,' he said.

She went into the nearby clump of trees.

'Hands behind you,' said the voice, as the man took a length of cord from his pocket.

'Turn around.'

She turned her back to him, her heart trying to hammer its way through her rib cage.

He started to tie her hands.

And now she made the move that she'd been working out all through the drive. She reached behind her with a leg sweep and cut her assailant's feet from under him.

He went crashing, the gun spinning away, but he ankle-tripped Maggie and brought her down, too.

Then the fight was on as they both scrambled to their feet, Maggie using every trick she had been taught to counter her opponent's weight and strength. She was fitter, but he was bigger and stronger. He was also maniacal. She felt herself being worn down. She threw him again and tried to run, but he reached out a hand and grabbed her calf, bringing her down again.

Almost as a reflex, she grabbed for his hood and ripped it off; it might somehow make him more vulnerable. There was a moment's frozen pause:

'Stringer!' she said.

'It's only in stories that the obvious is misleading,' he said. 'I wish you hadn't done that, lady law.'

'Why me?' she asked, trying to keep him talking. She knew , despairingly, that Jake had lost her.

'I've seen you around,' he said. 'I've always fancied you. But policewomen *are* difficult.'

She scrambled to her feet, but he took an iron grip on her hands, forcing her back against a tree. 'You shouldn't have taken the hood off,' he said. 'It needn't have been like this. But now I've no choice.'

He transferred his hands to her throat and started to squeeze. She tried to knee him in the groin, but he was ready for that.

His hands started to tighten. She tried to find his little fingers, in order to twist them.

On the road, Croft, breathing deeply to keep his hands steady against mounting panic, swept the darkened park with the night 'scope, yard by yard.

The hands tightened, the black eyes stared, mercilessly gloating into Maggie's face. Her blood started to pound in her ears. She started to slide slowly down the trunk of the tree.

Then Croft got it. In the eerie green glow which the light-enhancer produced, he saw the bizarre scene outlined:

'Over there!' he yelled.

They leapt into their cars and, headlights blazing, sirens screaming, mounted the pavement and roared across the grass.

Jimmy left the car like a cruise missile and launched himself, two feet off the ground, head first at Stringer, the impact tearing Stringer's hands from Maggie's throat, as Maggie collapsed on the ground.

Stringer fought like an animal, but, in the end, it was Jake and Croft's sergeant who had to pull Jimmy off him to prevent Jimmy killing him.

Croft was bending over Maggie, gently patting her face, loosening her clothes, his face very close to hers.

Her eyes opened suddenly like a doll's and looked straight into his: 'I think that will be all, Inspector.' she said, drily.

The realisation dawned: 'What are you doing here, anyway?' she demanded.

Croft grinned: 'Someone should tell your team about back doors,' he said.

Maggie tried to swallow her humiliation, except that swallowing was going to be a bit difficult for the next few days:

'Thanks . . . Bob,' she smiled.

Christ, heads were going to roll tomorrow!

DEEP BENEATH THE SEA
A DEADLY TRAP AWAITS . . .

SEA LEOPARD

Craig Thomas

The British nuclear submarine *HMS Proteus* carries the most sophisticated anti-detection equipment in the world. Codenamed 'LEOPARD', the top-secret anti-sonar systems render *Proteus* undetectable to the Russians. Sea trials completed, *Proteus*' first mission is to chart the new Soviet underwater defence system which poses the most deadly threat to NATO's northern flank.

But *Proteus* picks up a distress signal. From a Soviet submarine lying crippled on the sea floor. And as she sets out on her rescue mission the Russians prepare to spring a devastating deathtrap twenty fathoms beneath the ocean . . .

ADVENTURE/THRILLER 0 7221 8453 0 £1.95